Kira

DOWN UNDER

By Erin Teagan

★ AmericanGirl®

Published by American Girl Publishing

21 22 23 24 25 26 27 QP 12 11 10 9 8 7 6 5 4 3

This book is a work of fiction. Any similarity to real persons, living or dead,
is coincidental and not intended by American Girl. References to real events,
people, or places are used fictitiously. Other names, characters, places,
and incidents are the products of imagination.

All American Girl marks and Kira™ are trademarks of American Girl.

Illustrations by Millie Liu
Cover image by Millie Liu · Book design by Gretchen Becker

The following individuals and organizations have generously granted permission
to reproduce their photographs: pp. 125—129—courtesy of Alison & Timothy Bee;
pp. 130—131—courtesy of Patty Schuchman Photography, LLC. All rights reserved;
courtesy of Erin Teagan; pp. 132—133—courtesy of Erin Teagan; iStock.com/mlharing.

Cataloging-in-Publication Data available from the Library of Congress

FOR CADEN

—E.T.

WILDLIFE

Holding some of our foster kitties!
Kira + Mom
xoxo

Clinic

Mrs. Curry

Mr. Curry

Alexis

SOFT RELEASE THIS WEEK: DODGER

Lynette + Mamie's Wedding

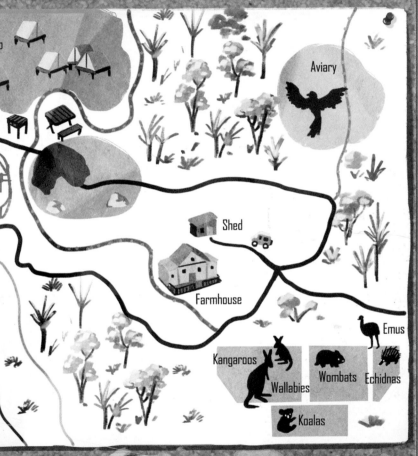

SCUE CLINIC

Aviary

Shed

Farmhouse

Emus

Kangaroos

Wombats

Echidnas

Wallabies

Koalas

PhD Student
Shashi

PhD Student
Evie

WITH GRATITUDE TO:

Alison Bee
Doctor of Veterinary Medicine
Queensland, Australia

Tassin Barnard
Walkabout Wildlife Park
New South Wales, Australia

Amelia Lachal and Libby McEniry
Mattel Australia
Victoria, Australia

CONTENTS

READY

Chapter 1

We walked across the town center toward the animal shelter, Mom carrying most of the foster kittens in their carrier. I held the littlest one, Nugget, who was my favorite.

"But, Mom, he's so tiny," I said. "Are you sure we can't keep him?"

"Kira—"

"I know. I know." It was the worst part about fostering kittens: bringing them back to the shelter so they could find their forever homes. Because after spending a few weeks with them, I just couldn't help but want their forever homes to be with me.

We passed the fountain where little kids splashed. The hot dog cart setting up for the day. The library. I checked my watch. Two minutes until ten o'clock, when my best friend and I always met at the statue of the lady holding a book on the first day of summer break. It was tradition. Except Laila wasn't coming this year. Not since she got a new best friend.

Mom must have caught me looking at the statue because

she said, "Here, hand me that kitten. I'll check them in. You go ahead and meet Laila."

Nugget snuggled into my neck. "I don't have anywhere to go, remember?"

Mom frowned. "Are you and Laila still arguing?"

"Mom," I said, "she doesn't want to be friends anymore." Laila only had time to be friends with the girls on her soccer team now. It was a fact of life. I was barely even offended anymore.

I opened the door to the animal shelter, cradling Nugget with my free hand.

"Okay, then you need to get yourself out there and make some *new* friends," Mom said, walking past me and depositing the carrier of mewing kittens on the counter.

I pulled Nugget to my chest and kissed his pink nose. "No thanks." Who needed human friends when you were surrounded by animals?

"Come on, Kira. Be social," Mom said. "You're going into fifth grade soon. You'll be at the middle school."

"So?" I hit the bell on the counter that said "Ring for service," hoping to end this conversation.

2

"Middle school is not an easy transition," Mom began, "especially if you're fighting with your best friend—"

Just because Mom teaches middle school, she thinks she knows everything about it.

Ms. Steph appeared, rolling a crate of long-eared puppies in front of her. "Sorry to keep you waiting, ladies!" Her four-year-old son vaulted into the room behind her, kicking and karate-chopping and nearly flailing into a bin of clean kitty litter. "Shhhh, Dougie," she said. "The kitties are sleeping. See?" She pointed to the little one purring on my shoulder. "By the way, congratulations, Miss Middle Schooler." She gave me a sideways hug. "Are you ready for your big adventure tomorrow?"

She was talking about how Mom and I were going to visit my great-aunts, who lived all the way across the world in Australia. They had a wildlife sanctuary and animal clinic where they rescued injured animals. Australia was bursting with animals that you couldn't find anywhere else in the world: pygmy possums that fit in the palm of your hand, kangaroos and wallabies, wombats and koalas, and birds of every color. We'd be there for two weeks. I wished we could stay for the whole summer. In fact, I wished we could just *move* there. Then I could be with animals twenty-four-seven and wouldn't have to go to middle school with my non-friend Laila.

Dougie did a series of spins and air punches, finishing with a roundhouse kick directly into a tower of dog bowls. The tower exploded, bowls rolling in all directions.

"Are you sure you can't stay here and babysit Dougie for me?" Ms. Steph asked with a groan. Then she smiled and went into the back office to get the kittens' paperwork.

"I remember when I first got to middle school," Mom said, launching right back into my least favorite topic. "I had a real hard time coping with the lockers." She looked at me sympathetically. "Or are you worried about the schedule and finding your classes? Or all the new people?"

"I just think if I'm going to be a veterinarian like Aunt Mamie, I should get a ton of experience working with animals," I said as I helped Dougie collect the scattered dog bowls. "Maybe I could stay in Australia and help Aunt Mamie in the clinic. I could do middle school online," I added. "People do that, you know. It's a thing."

She wasn't buying it. "Well, it's not a 'thing' in our family, Kira," Mom said, wincing as Dougie restacked the bowls into a teetering tower. "Maybe you should try and make up with Laila. You two have been best friends since kindergarten. You can't throw that kind of friendship away."

We tried at first to all be friends, Laila and me and the other soccer girls. But they only wanted to watch soccer or play soccer or talk about soccer, and I only wanted to do the stuff Laila and I used to do, like play with the kittens or hop on the rocks in the creek and look for frogs. And then once when I wanted to walk to the smoothie place instead of kicking the ball around, Laila said, in front of everyone, "Why can't you just go with the flow, Kira? You can never just relax and hang out. *That's* your problem."

And, as a matter of fact, I pretty much never wanted to hang out with her again after that.

Mom's phone rang. "It's Aunt Mamie and Auntie Lynette!" She accepted the video call, and my aunts' faces came into focus.

"Do you have any new joeys?" I asked right away.

"Well, hello to you, too," Auntie Lynette said, grinning.

"In fact, we do," Aunt Mamie said. "This one, you have to see for yourself." She leaned over a little pen, and we could see a basket with a blanket inside. She moved the blanket aside, and we saw a tiny sleeping koala, its arms wrapped tightly around a teddy bear.

"Awwwwww! Look!" I held the phone up for Mom and Dougie to see.

We all oohed and aahed until Auntie Lynette exclaimed, "Crikey, do you hear yourselves?"

"We can't help it!" I said, because loving animals ran in our family, and that meant we couldn't resist a cute animal.

And this little one was the cutest.

Auntie Lynette's face filled the phone. "I found a giant heap of kangaroo dung today. You want to see that, too?"

"Yes, please!" Dougie shouted.

"She's talking about poo, Dougie," I said, and he screeched and ran off.

Aunt Mamie took the phone back. "This little joey's in quarantine for a few more days to make sure he doesn't have any contagious diseases, but he should be in the clinic by the time you get here." She covered the koala back up.

"Have you named him yet?" I asked.

"Not yet. You have one in mind?"

I thought for a moment. My dad used to call me Bean, because he said I was just a little bean when I was born. He died three years ago, when I was seven, but this was one of the things I still remembered.

"How about Bean?" I suggested. "Because he's so small."

Aunt Mamie brightened. "You know, that's the perfect name for him. He's like a little bouncing bean."

Ms. Steph came back into the room to get the kittens, and I returned the phone to Mom. Gently, I put Nugget back in the box with his mewing sisters and brothers. "Don't cry," I said, giving them each a kiss on their fuzzy little heads. "You'll all find nice homes, and don't worry about me—I'll be in Australia taking care of the animals there." I patted the feisty black and white one. "And no biting, Mr. Spots. Families don't like it when you bite their kids, no matter how cute you are."

Ms. Steph leaned over the box with me.

"Just preparing them for their future," I said.

"Thank you for that," she said with a smile.

I spent a lot of time preparing for stuff. I knew how important it was to be prepared.

I heard Mom saying goodbye to Aunt Mamie and Auntie Lynette. "I can hardly wait another minute. See you on Monday!" Aunt Mamie said.

Even though we were leaving on a Friday, with the time change and huge distance between Michigan and Australia, it would be Monday when we arrived in Brisbane.

"Safe travels!" Ms. Steph called as we left the animal shelter.

Mom turned to me once we were outside. "Ready for this?"

Two weeks in Australia taking care of animals and visiting my favorite aunts of all time?

I nodded. I'd never been more ready for anything.

WELCOME TO AUSTRALIA
Chapter 2

The next day we had a twenty-two-hour plane ride. To pass the time, I read and reread my book of five thousand Aussie facts. We'd been in the air for about ten hours when I made friends with the boy across the aisle while we were eating our Tim Tams, an Australian cookie of chocolatey goodness, that came with our in-flight dinners.

"Just so you know," I told him, "there are more animals that can kill you in a heartbeat in Australia than anywhere else in the world."

"The whole *world*?" the boy asked, wide-eyed, chocolate crumbs all over his mouth. I hoped he would wipe them off before putting his mask back on.

I nodded, holding up my book of facts. "They've got funnel web spiders, box jellyfish, a tiny octopus that can give you a heart attack, and something called a cassowary, which is actually a really huge bird. Also, they have, um . . ." I flipped through my book. "Oh yeah, quokkas. Are you going to any islands in Western Australia?" The boy shrugged, stuffing another cookie into his mouth. "Well, it says here that even though quokkas look like smiling teddy bears"—

I showed him a picture—"they can bite."

"I don't remember being in so much danger the last time we were in Australia," Mom said.

"These are real facts, Mom," I said. I turned back to the boy. "Plus, did you know Australia has huge wildfires? Last year, one fire was the size of Europe!"

Above her mask, Mom gave me a look that meant, *That's enough.*

I stopped sharing my knowledge with the boy, but my thoughts didn't stop. "Do you think Aunt Mamie has anti-venom?" I asked Mom. "Because it says here there haven't been any deaths since they invented antivenom. For funnel web spiders at least."

"The word is *antivenin*, and I'm sure Aunt Mamie has treatments at hand for all kinds of bites and stings," Mom assured me. "Living out in the bush, she has to be prepared for anything."

That was another way I was like my great-aunt Mamie. Because I like to be prepared, too.

My aunts live out in the wilderness, which in Australia is known as *the bush*. Their place used to be the Bailey Farm, a big property that had been in my dad's family for genera-tions. When my grandmother and great-aunt Mamie were girls, they lived there. After they grew up, Aunt Mamie took over the property. She turned the barn into a veterinary clinic and let the farmland go wild. Now, Aunt Mamie ran the veterinary clinic and Auntie Lynette, a scientist, was in charge of the wilderness park, where animals can live safely and be studied by college students.

The question, though, was whether *people* could live safely with so many deady animals lurking about. How ready was I, really, for life in the bush?

When the plane landed in Brisbane, it was Monday morning. A driver met us and drove us for hours into the dusty countryside. I was tired after so much traveling but I stayed awake as long as I could, watching the dry landscape glowing golden in the late morning sun. We were supposed to visit last summer, but then major fires swept through the area, getting so close to the sanctuary that my aunts almost had to evacuate the animals. And then after that came the coronavirus and we weren't allowed to travel. We had to postpone our trip for a year.

"Look!" I yanked on Mom's shirt. Two kangaroos hopped along with us, as if to welcome us to their country.

It was afternoon by the time we turned onto the gravel driveway of the Bailey Wildlife Sanctuary. Auntie Lynette and Aunt Mamie were waiting for us. The car had barely stopped before we poured out of it and into their arms.

"Oh, we're so delighted to have you here," Aunt Mamie said, hugging me. "Does it look familiar? Do you remember it from when you were here three years ago?"

I nodded. The big white house next to the driveway was the farmhouse where Grandma and Aunt Mamie were sisters growing up. Down a path I could see the animal clinic. It was all familiar. I took a breath, so happy to be back.

"Is Bean still in quarantine?" I asked Aunt Mamie, taking my duffel bag out of the car.

"He gets out later tonight," she replied with a smile.

"How about we drop these bags off and enjoy a nice cup of tea on the veranda?" said Auntie Lynette.

I wanted to ask when we could go visit the animals at the clinic, but I waited patiently while the adults drank their tea. I sat on the steps and watched kangaroos nibbling on grass and wallabies chasing each other on the lawn. Giant ostrich-like emus strolled around, one sticking its long blue neck between the rails to greet me, probably looking for a treat. I thought of Dad and how much he had loved it here, too.

The adults talked about droughts and heat and fire seasons. Auntie Lynette, who is also a professor, was saying things like, "Even photosynthesis in leaves can be affected by hot, dry conditions . . ." My eyelids started to droop.

I felt a hand on my back. "Want to meet the animals?" Aunt Mamie asked.

"Yes!" I stood up, shaking the sleep from my body.

"I thought so. I'm taking Kira for a little walk," Aunt Mamie called to Mom, and we hit the path to the animal clinic, just the two of us.

Outside the clinic were a series of enclosures made of wood and chicken wire. Aunt Mamie put her nose up to the first pen. "G'day, Dodger, how's my darling this morning?" she said as a black and white bird waddled out of a shadowy corner. "Dodger's our magpie. Came in with a broken wing three months ago, and now he's ready for release."

"Today?" I said.

"Yes, and I'm going to miss him. Right, Dodger?" She turned to me. "I reckon it's the happiest and saddest day for an animal rescuer. Hardest part of the job is letting something go that you've come to love." She looked back at the bird. "My sweet Dodger. You'll be quite fine out there, I know."

"When will you release him?" I asked.

Aunt Mamie started walking again. "Tonight. We'll just open his cage and let him go as he pleases. It's called a soft release."

She stopped in front of the next enclosure. "This is Mum, our female koala. When she came to us, she had a tiny joey in her pouch, but unfortunately the baby didn't survive."

Mum was a ball of gray fur curled into the crook of a tree, her large talon-like claws holding tight to a leafy branch. "Whoa," I said. "Those are some serious claws."

Aunt Mamie laughed. "Koalas are territorial. If she were in the wild, she'd use them for defense. Our Mum, though, has barely any eyesight left and is a gentle beastie. I'm afraid she wouldn't stand much chance out in the wild."

"So you can't release her? Ever?" I asked. "She's all by herself. Doesn't she need a friend?"

"Koalas are solitary animals. She's happy as pie up there on her own with all the eucalyptus leaves she can eat." Aunt Mamie patted my hand. "She's got a few mates, though," she added, pointing to a small spikey creature shuffling across the floor of the enclosure.

What were those things called again? I knew it was an odd name. I racked my brain until it came back to me. "Echidna, right?" I asked.

"Right." Aunt Mamie smiled. "There are two of them running around in here. They make the perfect companions for Mum. She stays up high, and they stay low."

I watched the echidna scratch its way underneath a small bush growing out of the dry and sandy floor of the pen. It looked like a hedgehog mixed with a porcupine and an anteater.

"Echidnas are ferocious diggers," Aunt Mamie added, starting toward the next enclosure.

"Will the echidnas stay here forever, too?" I asked.

Aunt Mamie shook her head. "They'll eventually be released. Our animals start off inside the clinic for medical attention. Then the larger ones move to an outdoor enclosure while they finish recovering, and finally, when they're ready, they're released back to the wild," she explained. "Every so often we'll get a case like Mum, but our goal is for all our patients to return to their wild habitat."

At the next pen, I halted in front of a creature that looked like a bear cub, but with stubbier legs. It was lying in the middle of its pen, belly up to the sun, paws resting on its chest. A wombat.

"G'day Muffin, my girl," Aunt Mamie called into the enclosure. "Enjoying the sun, I see."

We had reached the door to the clinic. "Make sure to close the door behind you," said Aunt Mamie as we stepped inside. "We don't want any snakes in here, unless they're coming in for treatment."

Right. We were in Australia. Venomous spiders. Deadly snakes. I had to stay on guard. "Do you have antivenin?" I asked, trying to sound conversational.

"Of course we do," Aunt Mamie said, wiping her feet on the mat. "But working with animals always carries risks, Kira. You can't let fear of the worst keep you from living your best."

I thought about that. "Maybe, but it would be hard to live your best if you're in the hospital with a funnel web spider bite."

Aunt Mamie chuckled. "Pretty sure you missed my point, dearie."

I grinned. Of course I knew what she meant. I was just joking. Sort of.

ALEXIS

Chapter 3

Good afternoon everyone!" Aunt Mamie said as we walked into the animal clinic. "Food preparation is in full swing, I see."

In the middle of a big room, at a large steel table, several older teenagers in green smocks were chopping up carrots, squashes, apples, and heads of lettuce.

"These are our student trainees," Aunt Mamie said. "They're students from the university where your Auntie Lynette teaches environmental science. They work here a few hours a week as part of their studies."

Along the wall behind the trainees was an industrial sink, a huge double-door refrigerator, and a row of chalk-boards with food instructions: mealworms and oats for the bandicoots, seeds and mixed nuts for the parrots, no fruit peels or citrus for the bats. The other side of the room held aquariums and cages for small animals, and a rocking chair. At the far end were two doors labeled "Nursery" and "Exam Room."

Just as Aunt Mamie caught a squash about to roll off the table, the door banged behind us, and a girl rushed into the clinic. Behind her was a woman wearing a Bailey Wildlife Sanctuary work shirt and carrying a small wooden box.

"We found an injured bilby out in the bush," the girl said, out of breath. She looked about my age and wore cargo pants and a T-shirt that said, "I brake for wombats."

"It's got some lacerations," the woman added, handing the box to Aunt Mamie. Inside it, I glimpsed a furry gray animal the size of a baby bunny, with a long nose and big ears. "Must have been attacked by something."

Aunt Mamie peered at the bilby. "Looks like stitches will be needed," she said, and they went into the exam room.

The girl turned to me. "Are you Kira?" she asked. She had a long braid down her back and an explosion of freckles across her nose. "I'm Alexis Curry. I work here."

"You do?" I asked, impressed. "How old are you?"

"Almost eleven. My mum's the vet nurse," she said, motioning toward the exam room door. "And my dad's the ranger here. He takes care of the grounds and also does lots of the cooking. We live in the bush camp."

"What bush camp?" I asked, because the last time I was here, there was nothing called a bush camp. But before she could answer, her mother peeked out of the exam room.

"Alexis, can you take Blossom, please?" She held out a large canvas shoulder bag.

Alexis took the bag and opened it so I could see inside. At the bottom, two pointy ears stuck out of a knit pouch. "Ever bottle-feed a joey?"

I knew a joey was any kind of baby marsupial, but I was pretty sure this little one was a kangaroo. "No," I said, following her to the rocking chair, "but I've fed kittens with an eyedropper."

"Want to try feeding Blossom?" Alexis grabbed a bottle off the counter. "She's really sweet. Here, sit in the rocker."

I sat, and she lifted Blossom out of the canvas bag, still in her knit pouch, and set her in my lap, and then handed me the bottle. I gazed down at the baby kangaroo, her big dark eyes melting my heart. I offered the bottle, and she took it easily, clutching my hand with one of her tiny black paws, as if she was afraid I'd pull the bottle away. "She's adorable," I murmured.

"I know," Alexis agreed. "She's one of my favorites, aren't you, Blossom?" Alexis leaned over and stroked between the little kangaroo's ears. "Last week a roo got hit by a car, and this little joey was still in her pouch. Without her mum, she needs our help to survive. Joeys feel safest in their

mum's pouch, so we carry her around all the time in this."
Alexis held up the canvas shoulder bag. "Basically, this is
her new pouch, and my mum is her new mum. Aunt Mamie
says I get to raise the next joey myself, so I've been practic-
ing on Blossom, feeding her and carrying her when my
mum is busy. Hey, do you like wombats?"

Without waiting for an answer, Alexis turned and went
into the other room. Through the open door I glimpsed
wooden crates, piles of folded blankets, and more pouches
hanging on hooks. It was a joey nursery!

I felt a pang of envy. This girl, Alexis, was basically living the life I had always wanted . . . at my aunts' sanctuary.
And did she call Aunt Mamie "Aunt," too?

Alexis came back carrying a much smaller wombat
than Muffin. "This is Boomer," she told me. "He's almost
ten months old. Although his name should be Bonkers, if
you ask me." She put Boomer on the floor and he took off,
zigzagging across the tile and bulldozing through a bucket,
sending veggie scraps everywhere.

"Boomer!" Alexis scolded, bending over to pick up the
mess. She sat cross-legged on the floor and patted the tile
in front of her. "Over here!" she called. Boomer scurried
around the table and ran full tilt back to her, crawling into
her lap. But then a moment later, he flipped back onto the
floor and scampered over to a pile of folded towels on a low

shelf. Alexis tried to reach him before he toppled them over, but she was too late.

I couldn't help laughing, startling Blossom.

"Oh, Boomer, you naughty thing," Aunt Mamie said, coming out of the exam room, her hands on her hips.

Behind her, Mrs. Curry was placing the bilby, bundled in a blanket, into a cage along the wall.

"Will the bilby be okay?" I asked, pulling the empty bottle away from Blossom and rocking her back and forth.

"He has quite a few lacerations," Aunt Mamie said, "but I'm hopeful he'll make a full recovery. Poor thing was definitely attacked by something."

Alexis stood up, wiping her hands on a towel. "Something like a predator?"

Her mother nodded. "There might be a breach in the perimeter fence. I'll have your dad take a look."

I turned to Aunt Mamie. "I don't remember a fence around the property," I said.

"We've made a few changes since you were here last, Kira, including a bush camp for more staff and researchers," Aunt Mamie explained. "And also a fence to keep our animals safe from foxes and other predators."

"The bilby got lucky," said Mrs. Curry. "He could have been killed. I worry, though, that if there's a predator on the property, how many more animals will get hurt."

"Want me to go look for it?" Alexis offered. "How about tonight, when predators are most active?"

"No way, Alex," her mother said. "You're not to go skidding around the property in the dark looking for predators."

Alexis slumped. "But Kira could come with me. Right, Kira?"

She looked at me, clearly hoping for an ally. But traipsing through the Australian wilderness, in the dark, looking for dangerous animals, did not sound fun.

Suddenly Mrs. Curry rushed over to me, beaming. "Kira!" She shook my hand, bobbling around the sleepy joey in my arms. "Welcome! I've heard so much about you. We're so glad you're here!"

"Me, too," I told her, hoping Alexis would drop the idea of a predator hunt.

I was saved by Aunt Mamie. "Listen, girls, there is a rule here on the property," she said, looking stern. "No nighttime bush walks without an adult. Understand?"

"Sounds like a great rule," I said quickly. You weren't going to catch *me* out there in the dark with a predator on the loose, that was for sure.

"Fine," Alexis grumbled. "Well, hey—do you want to see the bush camp, Kira?"

"Sure!" I handed Blossom to Aunt Mamie. And then Alexis grabbed my hand and we were off.

BUSH CAMP
Chapter 4

We ran through the animal clinic and out the back door and onto a dirt path, dodging kangaroos and wallabies and something I thought was a snake but turned out to be a twisty branch. The path wound into a cluster of trees.

I put the brakes on. "Wait." Alexis looked at me. "What about funnel web spiders and brown snakes?"

"It's winter here," Alexis said. "We don't really see a lot of them now."

"What do you mean, it's winter?" I asked, confused. For one thing, this was nothing like the winter I knew. There were green leaves on the trees, and the air was warm in the sunshine. For another, it was June.

"Our winter is from June to September," Alexis told me. "It's a lot cooler, so spiders and snakes aren't hanging about the way they do in the summer, when it's hot."

"All right." I took a calming breath. I would trust the expert—for now. I followed her into the trees, along a path that led us to a small clearing with a circle of tents around a fire pit.

Alexis opened her arms wide. "Here's the bush camp.

This is where my parents and I live and where scientists stay when they're doing research here."

"Wow," I said, looking around. The large tents were on sturdy platforms, and it looked like they even had running water. I felt another twinge of envy. "What a fun place to live. You're so lucky!"

"Come meet my dad," Alexis said, leading me around the nearest tent and past a long picnic table, where a man in a khaki ranger uniform was cleaning a big outdoor grill. "Dad, this is Kira Bailey."

Mr. Curry looked up and wiped his hands on a towel. "Kira! Welcome!" he said, reaching out to shake my hand. "Hope you like sausages and prawns on the barbecue. Big dinner tonight, to welcome our new guests!"

A few hours later, we all gathered at the long picnic table. Besides Mom, Aunt Mamie, Auntie Lynette, and Mr. and Mrs. Curry, there was a younger-looking man sitting across from Alexis and me.

"Shashi is here from India to study frogs," Alexis told me. "He's a graduate student at the university."

We all sat down, and Aunt Mamie passed the bread. I was taking a roll for myself when a young woman appeared. She had a camera mounted to a tall tripod slung over her shoulder. "Hello, everyone!" she called.

"Hello, Evie! Time to call it a day?" Auntie Lynette replied. She turned to Mom and me. "Evie Charlesworth is one of my graduate students."

"Sorry to be late, mates," said Evie. "Caught sight of a white-browed babbler. Had to follow him through the bush until I got a good shot." She leaned her camera and tripod against a tree and sat down beside Shashi.

I passed Evie the bread. "Do you study frogs, too?" I asked her.

Evie smiled. "White-browed babblers are birds, not frogs," she said, taking a roll from the breadbasket and passing it to Shashi. "I'm the bird lady. I study ornithology."

"Evie and Shashi are working toward their PhDs," Auntie Lynette said to me. "It's the highest degree a scientist can achieve, and it takes a lot of research."

"This sanctuary is excellent for field research," Shashi said. "The river attracts a wide variety of amphibians."

"And birds. I logged sixteen parrot species today," Evie said. "You never know what you'll find out in the bush. Good thing last year's fires didn't reach the sanctuary."

"We're fortunate, indeed," agreed Aunt Mamie. "Let's hope our luck holds."

Auntie Lynette shook her head. "Everything's so dry with this drought, one lightning strike might be all it takes."

Mrs. Curry stood and picked up her plate. "Sorry to leave the party early, but it's time for Blossom's next feeding. She's growing like a weed. Be sure to eat your salad, love," she said to Alexis as she left the table.

"Aunt Mamie?" Alexis asked. "Remember how you said I could take care of the next joey we got? Does that mean I get to raise Bean all by myself?"

I felt a prick in my heart. Was she talking about my Bean?

Aunt Mamie took a sip of water. "Koala orphans can be a bit tricky, Alexis. Perhaps we should wait for the next joey."

"Oh." Alexis sat back, forking a piece of sausage. "Okay. Sure."

Relief flooded through me. Of course, I hadn't officially met Bean yet. But I had named him, and that made him feel like he was mine.

Aunt Mamie smiled at us. "You know, girls, between Blossom, Boomer, Bean, and the wallabies we took in from the Blue Mountain bushfire in New South Wales, we're going to need all the help we can get. There are plenty of jobs to go around, and I reckon you two will make a great team."

Alexis nodded enthusiastically. "Yes, we have loads in common! We both like animals—"

"We're both ten," I chimed in.

"And we both like prawns and sausages!" She pointed to our empty plates as evidence. "Hey, I have an idea—you should stay with me in my tent! Do you want to?" And then before I could answer, she leaned over the table and called, "Dad, can Kira share my tent?"

"Sure, possum, whatever you'd like," Mr. Curry called back.

"Can I, Mom?" I asked.

Mom was standing up, clearing her plate from the table. "If Kira's up for it, then it's okay with me."

"Well?" Alexis turned to me, holding up her crossed fingers.

"Yes!" I said, thrilled that she had invited me. We fist-bumped to seal the deal.

As Mr. Curry passed around sponge cake and strawberries for dessert, I sighed with contentment. I was with my favorite aunts at their beautiful sanctuary, surrounded by adorable animals, with a new friend, maybe even a new *best* friend. I never wanted to leave.

ROOMMATES
Chapter 5

Alexis and I left the table and headed for the tents. We passed the Wombat, Magpie, and Dingo tents, and stopped in front of the one named Wallaroo. I followed Alexis up the three wooden steps onto a little private front porch. She unzipped the tent and held it open. "See? Plenty of room for the two of us."

"Wow," I said as we stepped inside. "This is amazing!" It was not a regular tent—it was like a bedroom in the middle of the wilderness, with a fluffy area rug, a twin-size bed with a purply-blue comforter and koala pillows. There was even a washbasin and mirror on the back wall.

Alexis bounced onto her bed. "Your cot can go here, by the window. Just so you know, there's a light outside that turns on every once in a while. It's motion sensored and might pick up a roo or two."

I grinned. "I don't mind that." Kangaroos hopping around my tent while I slept? No big deal. But then my mind started thinking about other creatures that might creep in the night. "Um, do you ever get snakes or goannas coming into your tent?"

Alexis cleared a floor cushion and a stack of books from the area where my bed would go. "Nope. Just make sure you keep the door zipped up."

I looked at our door, which was flapping slightly in the breeze, wide open for any venomous creature to use.

"Do you worry a lot?" asked Alexis, tossing a pile of clothes into a hamper.

"Me? Um, well . . . I like to be prepared is all," I told her.

"Me, too," she said. "Once we had to take a really long bush walk to find a hurt wallaby, and I brought exactly enough pieces of gum to last the whole trip without losing flavor. *That* took careful planning."

I nodded as if I agreed, but honestly if I were about to go on a daylong bush walk, I'd bring special pads for blisters, binoculars so we could keep an eye out for dangers ahead, a compass so I wouldn't get lost, and my edible plants of Australia chart in case we had to survive a few days in the wild.

"Let's get all the stuff we need before dark," said Alexis. "Everything is at the farmhouse."

I followed her out of the tent and carefully zipped the flap closed behind me.

At the farmhouse, Aunt Mamie and Auntie Lynette were drinking tea in the kitchen with Mom. They took us to the basement, where they had a storage room full of camping

gear. Auntie Lynette pulled out a folded camp cot for me, and Aunt Mamie gathered a sleeping bag and pillow.

"Give them all a good shake," she said, "just in case of critters."

"What?" I gasped, horrified.

"Oh, bite your bum," Auntie Lynette said, waving me off. "Can't be scared of critters when you live in the bush."

Aunt Mamie spotted Alexis looking at a box on one of the shelves. "Take anything you want from here, girls," she said, placing it on the floor for us. "Decorations from our wedding."

Aunt Mamie and Auntie Lynette had been my aunties since before I was born, but they only got married a few years ago, after the law was changed to allow it. The wedding was shortly after my dad died, so it was too hard for Mom and me to come.

"We wish your family could have been there, Kira," Aunt Mamie said softly.

"I was there!" Alexis piped up, rifling through a bunch of silk flowers.

Aunt Mamie gave me a hug. "You were there in our hearts, bunny." And then Auntie Lynette hugged us hard together, almost knocking us over and making us all laugh.

Alexis pulled a long flowy purple curtain out of the

box. "Ooh, I love this. Purple's my favorite color. Do you like it, Kira?" She swished it around, spinning.

"Yeah! We could drape it across the front of the tent like a dramatic entrance," I said. And so we took the purple curtain along with the cot, sleeping bag, and blanket, and set up our own room in the bush camp.

Then we joined the Currys, Shashi, and Evie at the barbecue to make a damper, which I learned was soda bread cooked in hot ashes. You eat it dipped in honey. It was pretty much the best night of my life.

As we walked back to our little porch, we admired the tent. A lantern made the tent and purple curtain glow. "It looks so pretty and cozy," I said with a sigh. "My friend from home would love it."

"You should take a picture and send it to her. I'll even be in it." Alexis hopped onto the porch and struck a pose.

"Actually, um, we're not really friends anymore," I said.

Alexis dropped her arms. "Why not?"

"It's weird," I said, walking past her into the tent and sitting on the edge of my cot.

"I love weird stuff. Try me," Alexis urged.

So I told her the whole story. How Laila dropped me when she got serious about soccer and found a whole new group of friends. "The last time we hung out," I said, looking at my feet, "I wanted to walk to the smoothie shop, something we used to do all the time, but she just wanted to kick the soccer ball around. All the girls did, except for me. I'm not a big fan of soccer so I decided to go home. She got mad and said I needed to go with the flow and that's my whole problem." I stopped talking, realizing I had totally spilled my guts to her.

"Give me that," Alexis said, taking my phone. "Sounds like go-with-the-flow means do-what-she-wants-all-the-time. I've had those kinds of friends before. You deserve a better friend than that."

"Thanks, Alexis," I said, my heart swelling.

"You can call me Alex if you want," she said. "At least, that's what my friends call me." Then she put her arm over my shoulder, and we snapped a selfie in front of our tent.

BEAN

Chapter 6

W e were about to get into our pajamas when we heard a "Pssst" from outside. It was Aunt Mamie. "If you're still up," she called softly, "there's a little koala back at the clinic who just woke up, and I think he wants to meet you."

Alexis and I bolted out of the tent and up the path, looping back around to walk a bit with Aunt Mamie, who wasn't moving fast enough, and then racing off again. When we got to the clinic, Aunt Mamie raised a finger to her lips. "*Shhh.*" She tiptoed inside, and Alexis and I followed, grinning at each other.

Aunt Mamie brought us over to the nursery room. On the floor was a basket filled with blankets. She peeled back one of the blankets, and there was Bean, wide awake and holding tight to his stuffed bear.

"Awww!" Alexis and I gushed. On a scale from one to ten, this joey's cuteness factor was off the charts.

"Can we feed him?" Alexis asked, hooking her arm through mine. "Please?"

"We'll give it a try," Aunt Mamie said. "He's a bit of a fussy eater. He needs several good meals a day to grow properly, but he doesn't always get them."

"Kira can go first," Alexis said generously. "She's our guest, right, Aunt Mamie?"

I flushed. "I'm not really a guest. I'm family." I knew Alexis probably hadn't meant anything by it, but being called a guest made me feel left out. This property had been in the Bailey family—*my* family—for generations. Didn't that make *her* the guest? I kept those thoughts to myself, though. "Thanks, Alex, for letting me try first."

I settled into a rocking chair, and Aunt Mamie handed me the little koala, swaddled in his blanket and still clutching his teddy bear. Bean's fur was so soft, a mix of dark and light gray with a bit of white on his tufted ears. He blinked up at me with his big black eyes, and my heart melted.

"Tip his bottle just slightly," Aunt Mamie said.

A drip of formula landed on his mouth and he licked it off with his tiny pink tongue. "Great job, little Bean," I said. When I hovered the bottle over his mouth a second time, he took a messy drink.

"You're a natural with him, Kira," Aunt Mamie said. "He's taking the bottle so well with you."

When Bean was finished with his bottle, Aunt Mamie put him on the floor, tugged his teddy from his grasp, and slid it across the room. Bean bobbled after it. "He likes to play chase," she told us.

BEAN

"Can I try?" Alexis asked. She intercepted the teddy bear and tossed it in the other direction as Bean went to grab it. "Aww!" Alexis cooed. "He loves his teddy!"

"Don't koalas sleep about twenty hours a day?" I asked Aunt Mamie.

"Yes. The eucalyptus leaves they eat don't have a lot of nutrients, so when they're not eating, they're mostly sleeping," said Aunt Mamie. "But when he's awake, it's good for him to play and use his muscles."

When the teddy bear was close to me, I tossed it back toward Alexis, but Bean didn't run after it. "I think he's getting tired already," I said. Sure enough, Bean ignored his teddy and then slowly, one little leg at a time, crawled into my lap for a snuggle.

The next morning, I was up too early, not used to Australian time. The clock in our tent read five thirty. I tried counting to a thousand, willing myself back to sleep, but it was no use. I got up, careful not to wake Alexis.

It was still dark outside as I started down the path from the bush camp to the farmhouse. There were no lights on at the house—everyone was still asleep. So I settled into the porch swing on the veranda (after checking the cushions for creepy-crawlies) and watched the sky turn pink and gold.

I swung back and forth, remembering the last time I had watched the sunrise from this swing. Dad had been sitting beside me. I missed him, but it was a happy memory.

The sun was nearly up when I saw movement in a bush nearby, probably a kangaroo or a wallaby. Unless—could it be the fox? And did foxes ever attack humans?

I stopped swinging. The bush moved again, and I started planning my escape. Then a little nose and whiskers appeared. It was just a cat! I stayed still and silent, until it stepped all the way out of the bush. It was a little orange tabby. Not exactly the ferocious fox I had imagined.

"Here, kitty, kitty," I called softly. "Are you hungry?" I looked around for something to offer as the cat took cautious steps through the grass toward me, its tail twitching.

I slid off the swing. The cat froze, looking as if it might bolt, so I paused, giving it a chance to relax, and then moved a bit closer. As I slowly reached out my hand for it to smell, the farmhouse's screen door slammed, and the cat skittered out of sight.

BEAN

Mom and Auntie Lynette came down the steps of the veranda and joined me. "Getting in some morning calisthenics, are we?" Auntie Lynette asked, doing a dramatic leg stretch.

I laughed. "No, I just couldn't sleep."

"Me neither," Mom said, rubbing her eyes. "It takes a few days to get used to the time difference."

Auntie Lynette put her arm over my shoulder, and we started down the path to the bush camp, where Mr. Curry was already frying up breakfast.

"There you are!" Alex said, tying her shoes at the picnic table. "Ready to head over to the clinic?"

"Yep," I said. "Aunt Mamie is probably waiting for us."

"How about a brekky roll first?" Mr. Curry said.

"No time," Alexis said.

Mr. Curry fancy-flipped a piece of tomato, which landed on the ground. "Crikey!" An emu came over for a look, snapping it up in its beak. "I reckon you girls could take a minute for breakfast."

Alexis looked at me and groaned. "Dad. Gah. Fine. I'll have a piece of bacon."

"Sure thing, possum, with a side of egg and toast, if you don't mind." He turned over a fried egg and buttered two pieces of bread, tossing them onto the pan. "Kira? Tomato with yours?"

"No thanks, Mr. Curry. Smells delicious."

We sat down at the long wooden table across from Mom and Auntie Lynette, as three cockatoos flew overhead, their squawks echoing over the bush camp.

"Aunt Mamie said she wanted to give Boomer a lot of time outside today," Alexis said to me. "He's almost grown out of his baby box in the clinic."

"Does that mean he's ready for the big enclosure with Muffin?" I asked.

"Well, he's almost ten months old and he doesn't need a heat lamp or anything, so—"

"Alexis?" Mrs. Curry said, popping her head out of her tent. "I hear you making plans over there like you don't have schoolwork to do."

"Mum, I can do it later."

"You will do it straight after breakfast, thank you," her mother said firmly.

"Mum!" Alexis protested, but Mrs. Curry came all the way out of her tent with a look that meant serious business.

Alexis relented. "Brutal," she muttered to me.

I hadn't noticed a school when we drove in yesterday. "Where do you go to school?" I asked her.

"Online," Alexis replied, her mouth full, and I almost choked on my eggs. I turned to my mother.

"See, Mom? I told you, kids do school online all the time!"

Mom smiled patiently. "Yes, when they live on a wildlife sanctuary."

"Which I would, if you loved me and let me live here all the time." I shot her a grin, which she did not return. "Alex and I could be in the same class!"

"Oh, yes! Please, Mrs. Bailey?" Alexis begged.

Mom shook her head. "You're coming home with me in two weeks, Kira."

Alexis and I slumped.

Mom forked a piece of egg. "One day you'll thank me for making you go to middle school."

I laugh-snorted. "Pretty sure nobody in the history of the world has thanked their parents for sending them to middle school." Now I couldn't finish my breakfast. Here I was in the middle of the Australian bush, and my stomach was upset about a place on the other side of the planet.

"Well," Alexis said, standing up and taking her plate. "I'm off to do maths or whatever. I'll meet you later at the clinic, Kira."

"School ruins everything," I called after her.

"You can say that again!" She held up a fist in solidarity.

When she was gone, I turned to my mother. "Alexis has real jobs here, Mom, and she's my age. She gets to clean the enclosures and feed the animals, and Aunt Mamie said that she can raise the next joey they get. *Raise a joey. By herself.*"

Mom reached across the table, patting my hand. "Don't forget you have a great life back home in Michigan, Kira. Who would foster all those kittens?" I pulled my hand away. "Life isn't perfect on the sanctuary, either, Kira. I'm sure Alexis would tell you that. It's very hard work. And some of the animals don't make it. And remember all those bushfires in Australia last winter? Several weren't far from here. That must have been very scary."

"Yeah, but the fires didn't reach the sanctuary." I sighed. My mom just didn't get it. "It's like Alexis has the exact life I can only dream about. Going to school online. Taking care of animals all day. Hanging out with Aunt Mamie and helping her in the clinic."

Mom picked up my plate, stacked it on hers, and stood up from the table. "Appreciate what you have, Kira. We're here in Australia as guests of this amazing sanctuary for the next two weeks. How many ten-year-olds get to do that? Enjoy every minute of your good fortune, sweetheart."

As I watched Mom walk away, I couldn't help thinking that she was wrong.

I was more than just a guest. I belonged here.

INTO THE BUSH
Chapter 7

I spent the next few days being over-the-top helpful at the animal clinic with Alexis. When we weren't feeding Blossom, cuddling with Bean, or taking Boomer for walks outside, we were cleaning cages and pens, prepping food with the student trainees, doing dishes, or hanging laundry.

"How did you learn so much about taking care of animals?" Alexis asked me, wedging half an orange between two tree branches in the parrot enclosure.

"I foster kittens for an animal shelter back home," I said, placing my rake between my shoes and Dexter, the naughty cockatoo who liked to chew laces. "I also read a lot about animals. Everyone says that I take after Aunt Mamie. Like, it's in my blood or something."

"Hey, people say that about me, too!" Alexis said. "How I'm a lot like Aunt Mamie. I mean, I don't know if it's in my blood—"

"Yeah, because you're not related." I pushed a soggy banana onto a sharp twig coming out of a tree, regretting my words as soon as they left my mouth. I saw Alexis's smile falter. "Sorry . . . um, that came out wrong."

"No worries," she said quickly. "Aunt Mamie and Auntie Lynette say that everyone at the sanctuary is one big family. I like that part about living here. My own family is pretty small. Just me, my mum, and my dad." She raked a corner that was messy with leaves. "It would be loads better if you could stay here, too. It's nice having another kid around."

"That would be amazing," I said. "Believe me, I've already asked my mom to stay about a million times." I dropped some seeds into a cup, and Alexis tossed a piece of brown lettuce into the trash bucket. Dexter hopped over and toppled the entire bucket.

"You little bugger!" Alexis said, both of us laughing, shooing Dexter away so we could pick up the mess.

"Morning, ladies." It was Auntie Lynette, peering in from outside the fence. "Shashi and I are going for a drive to the other side of the property to install a piece of equipment. Want to come?"

We dropped what we were doing, saying goodbye to Dexter, who squawked as we left with the bucket. We dumped the contents into a wheelbarrow by the shed, where the emus would certainly find it. Then we followed Auntie Lynette back to the bush camp.

Shashi waited beside a land rover that had supplies strapped onto the roof rack and a giant snorkel attached to the hood.

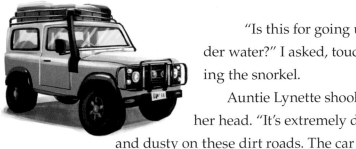

"Is this for going under water?" I asked, touching the snorkel.

Auntie Lynette shook her head. "It's extremely dry and dusty on these dirt roads. The car takes air through the snorkel to keep the dust out of the engine."

We all piled into the car and started down the skinny, rutted path, equipment rattling and water containers bouncing. We drove through dense woods over fallen branches, down into gullys and back up onto narrow roads past dry, grassy fields, and through shallow rivers so clear you could see the rocks at the bottom.

"Look! Wombat burrows!" Alexis pointed to a few wombat-size holes on a hill as we drove by.

In the front seat, Shashi asked Auntie Lynette, "Do you think we'll see any rain this month?"

"It's a tough drought, this one," Auntie Lynette said. "The fuel load is high. We're ripe for a fire."

I felt a twinge of worry. "What do you mean?"

"See how the forest floor is covered with dry leaves and dead timber? We call that fuel load, because it would fuel a bushfire." Auntie Lynette pointed out the window. "And do you see how much space there is between the trees here?

All the little shrubs that grow between the trees have been munched away by the animals, so all we have left is dry, highly flammable tree litter. It's dangerous."

Auntie Lynette said to Shashi, "I applied for a controlled burn last winter, but all the fireys were busy fighting wild bushfires, so we were never able to get our burn. I'm hoping we can get one done in the autumn."

"A controlled burn? You mean they'd set a fire on purpose?" I asked. "Here? At the sanctuary?"

"Yes, our rural fire brigade does controlled burns to get rid of the ground litter," Auntie Lynette replied. "As devastating as fire can be, some plants need the heat of fire for their seeds to germinate."

"Professor Mackie has been studying the effects of fire on plants for many years," Shashi told us.

"So what can we do?" I asked, feeling unsettled.

"We take precautions," said Auntie Lynette. "Hope for a good rain. And pray that a lightning strike doesn't set this bush on fire."

When we reached the far end of the property, we parked and got out of the land rover, feeling a bit sick from the rough ride. Alexis and I sat on a rock and sipped bubbly water, while Shashi and Auntie Lynette organized their equipment.

Two colorful birds zipped by us and landed in the tree above my head. "I don't think I'll ever get used to wild parrots just flying around like that," I said.

"Those are rainbow lorikeets," Alexis said, taking another gulp of water. "Pretty common."

"What about the red and purple ones over there?" I asked, pointing.

Alexis peered at them. "Crimson rosellas, I think."

"You know your birds, huh?" I took out my phone to take a picture of the parrots and spotted another one. "What about that bright blue and red one?"

Alexis sat up straighter, squinting at it. "You know, I'm not sure. Can you take a picture of it? We'll look it up in my bird book when we get back to camp."

But as soon as I brought my phone up to take a picture, the bird flew off, and I only got a blur of colors.

"Alexis! Kira!" Shashi called. "I could use a hand over here!"

We jogged over to a rock outcropping, where Shashi was pounding a metal stake into the ground by a series of little pools. "Hand me that, please?" He pointed to a small green device sitting on top of his bag.

"What is it?" I asked.

"A song meter, right?" Alexis asked him. "Are you recording frog sounds?"

The device was only a little bigger than my hand, with two microphones sticking out the sides like lollipops. Shashi picked it up and unlatched the front cover, revealing a control panel inside. He hung the device on the stake using zip ties and then said, "I programmed it to listen to sounds at night. My phone has an app that will name the different frog songs it picks up. Each species of frog has a different sound, so then we'll know what kinds of frogs live on this part of the property."

We walked a little ways along the path by the creek to install another song meter in a different area, passing Auntie Lynette, who was taking a clipping of a fern-like plant. Suddenly Alexis grabbed my arm. "Stop!" She pointed to the ground where I was about to step, and I saw a bunch of brown and black spines sticking out of the dirt.

Auntie Lynette came over. "It's an echidna."

I bent down for a closer look. The echidna was buried so far into the sandy earth that it looked like a spikey plant.

"See these tracks it made?" Auntie Lynette pointed to a line of small tracks in the dirt. The right foot made a nearly perfect impression of a paw with two little claws and two long claws, but the left foot made a rough line, as though it was dragging through the dirt. "I reckon this fellow is limping."

"Should we bring it into the clinic?" I asked.

INTO THE BUSH

Auntie Lynette expertly dug out the echidna and lifted it up in one hand as the little creature rolled itself into a ball. His side looked wet and blotchy red, and one leg hung limp.

"Looks like he's bleeding," said Alexis. "It's the predator again, isn't it?"

"I reckon so," Auntie Lynette said grimly. "Let's get back to the clinic. Shashi, you about ready?"

"I'll be there in a minute, Professor Mackie," said Shashi.

"Auntie," I asked as we returned to the land rover, "how many more injured animals do you think are out here that we don't even know about?"

"Hard to say. But if there's a fox," she answered, "depending on how long it's been lurking about the property, there could be many more injured."

"Or eaten," Alex added.

I sucked in a breath, checking over my shoulder for killer foxes, and then rushed for the safety of the land rover.

A VISIT WITH MUM
Chapter 8

When we got back to camp, Auntie Lynette drove straight to the animal clinic. Inside, we found Aunt Mamie and Mrs. Curry there with the student trainees, who were chopping up meat for the kookaburras.

"How we going?" Aunt Mamie came around the table, wiping her hands on her apron. "What do we have here?"

Alex and I held out a box. "An echidna," I said, holding out a box.

"Injured by the predator," Alexis added. "Probably."

Mrs. Curry looked up from her work. "How about you girls fill that empty cage over there with some leaves? We can move the little fellow in there after his checkup. Wear gloves, please." She pulled two pairs of gloves hanging off the sink and squeezed the tips of each finger. I heard a crunch.

"What was that?" I asked.

Mrs. Curry tipped the glove upside down and some-thing black and leggy fell out.

"Just a house spider—but always check first," she said. "And always wear gloves when raking leaves over by the shed. Funnel web spiders really like it over there."

I grimaced as Alex grabbed a pair of gloves and a bucket. "Coming, Kira?"

I hesitated.

She shook her head. "Um, are you okay?"

I swallowed. "Me? Oh, yeah, totally fine," I said, tamping down my fears. It didn't help that I knew from my research that funnel web spiders could be the size of a human hand. "I'm coming."

Aunt Mamie spoke from behind me. "Actually, Kira, I could use your help feeding Bean. Alexis, do you mind?"

I knew Alexis wasn't thrilled to get the job of collecting spider infested leaves instead of feeding a cuddly koala, but she gave Aunt Mamie a thumbs-up and took her bucket outside as if it was no big deal.

"After I get this echidna fixed up, we'll try Bean in the outdoor enclosure for a bit," Aunt Mamie added.

"You think he's ready for that?" I asked.

"Yes, and the sooner the better," she explained. "Sometimes adult females take to joeys, letting them attach to their backs like their own baby. We introduced Mum and Bean yesterday and Mum was friendly to him, so I'm hopeful they'll form a bond and she'll take him in and raise him."

Mrs. Curry and Aunt Mamie took the echidna to the exam room while I retrieved Bean from his little basket and sat in a rocking chair with his bottle. I kept Bean wrapped in his blanket with his teddy bear, just the way he liked it, and he took his bottle easily.

"That's my good boy," I murmured. "You need to eat to get big and strong." He looked up at me, a dot of formula on his nose. I wiped it off and kissed his soft head.

I had lunch at the farmhouse with Mom and my aunts. After we had eaten and cleaned up, Aunt Mamie said to me, "Let's go see if Mum is up for a visit."

Bean was sleeping when we arrived back at the clinic. I picked him up and we walked to Mum's pen. He looked so sweet and peaceful, I never wanted to let him go.

"Perfect, Mum's on a nice low branch," Aunt Mamie said when we reached the pen. She opened the gate, and we went in. "Here, I'll take Bean, and you take away his stuffy if you can."

I gave her Bean and shook the teddy bear out of his grip, which was not easy. Aunt Mamie brought Bean close to Mum, who sniffed him. He looked so tiny next to Mum.

My heart pounded, and I reminded myself that this was good for Bean. Bonding with Mum would give him his best chance at survival.

Aunt Mamie took her time attaching Bean to Mum's back, slowly letting go. At first, Bean slipped as if he was going to fall, and I could barely watch. But then he clutched the big koala's back and relaxed against her body. After a few minutes, Aunt Mamie stepped back a bit.

"It's important not to intervene in this bonding," she said softly to me. "But we have to make sure he's safe as well. We don't want him falling from the branch." She took another step back, and I felt a streak of worry. "We'll let Bean hang out here for a few minutes. I'm going to check on Mum's roommates." I knew she meant the two echidnas that shared Mum's pen. "Can you watch him?" I nodded. "Stand just far enough away so you don't distract him, but close enough to catch him if he falls."

I ducked under one of the branches to be closer to Bean, running through all possible scenarios of how and where he might fall so I could be prepared. I had to be ready if he needed me. I heard Aunt Mamie talking to one of the echidnas on the ground, and I slid one step closer to Bean. I was in charge of this little creature and I wasn't about to let anything happen to him.

When Bean opened his eyes and saw me and his teddy

bear, he perked up and pushed away from Mum. I tried to hide his teddy, but Bean was already crawling down the branch.

"No, Bean," I whispered. "Stay there." I tried to push him back up to Mum. Bean cried, flapping a little hand in my direction. I reached his teddy out for him to grab, and then took him off the branch and hugged him tight.

"Kira," Aunt Mamie called from across the enclosure, her voice strained.

I ducked under the branch to tell her what happened, holding Bean against my chest. I found Aunt Mamie holding one of the echidnas, but her hands were shaking and she was breathing heavily.

"Can you . . . I need . . ." Aunt Mamie gasped, her skin pale and sweaty.

"Aunt Mamie?" I asked. "Are you okay?" Just then Mrs. Curry walked by with a box of supplies. "I think we need help!" I called to her.

Mrs. Curry dropped the box and sprinted into the pen, catching the echidna before it fell.

And then Aunt Mamie collapsed onto the floor of the koala pen.

WAITING FOR NEWS
Chapter 9

Mom and Auntie Lynette followed the ambulance to the hospital. The rest of us tried to keep busy while we waited for news. After supper, Mr. Curry used his drone to look for breaches in the fence. Alexis went to do her school-work without being told. Shashi and Evie sat at the picnic table working on their laptops. And Mrs. Curry and I went back to the clinic area to check on the animals.

Walking by the pens, I saw stubborn Dodger the magpie still hanging out in his enclosure, even though the door was wide open. I gave Mum fresh eucalyptus leaves, cleaned and refilled the water bowls in the wombat pen, and gave Bean his evening bottle feeding. When I got back to the bush camp, I found Alexis on her bed, hunched over her schoolbooks.

"Do you have that bird book?" I asked her. She reached over and pulled a thick book out of the cubby by her bed and handed it to me. It was an illustrated guide to the birds of Australia. I flipped through it to the section on parrots. There was only one bird that looked like the parrot in my memory.

"Alex, I think I found it."
I held the book up to show
her the illustration. The
bird on the page was
called the paradise
parrot. Like the bird we
had seen, it was very colorful, mostly
blue and green, with black-edged wings and a
shock of red on the shoulder and under the tail. It was one
of the prettiest birds I'd ever seen.

Alexis swung her legs over her bed and sat up. "Yes,
there it is!" she exclaimed. "I'm sure that's the bird we saw."

"It says here they nest in termite mounds," I told her.

"Oh, we have loads of those around here," Alexis said.
"I'm telling you, that's the bird. Don't you think?"

"Yes, but wait," I said, reading further.

"What?" Alexis asked, coming over. "What's it say?"

I frowned. "These parrots have been extinct since 1927."

"No way," she said, taking the book and flipping
through the pages. "But there aren't any other birds in here
that look like the one we saw."

"I know," I agreed.

Alexis was quiet for a moment, staring at the picture.
"Maybe we should ask Evie about it."

"Or Aunt Mamie. She knows a lot about birds," I said.

"Except . . . we'd have to wait until she gets back from the hospital."

After that, we didn't feel much like talking. We tried staying up until Mom and my aunts came home, but eventually we shut off our lights and went to sleep.

Alexis and I both woke up early the next morning. We found Mr. Curry already up and at the grill, so we dragged our blankets outside and joined him.

"Did my mom come home last night?" I asked.

He nodded. "Heard them pull in real late. They said the hospital admitted Mamie and was running tests."

"What kind of tests?" Alexis asked.

"We'll have to wait for more details, sweetheart," her father said.

"Is she okay?" Alexis persisted. "How bad is it? When will she come home?"

"Possum," Mr. Curry said, "patience."

Alexis's eyes were welling up, and I swallowed the lump in my throat, trying hard to keep my own worry from spilling out. I tried not to think of my father, who never came home from the hospital.

Soon Shashi and Evie joined us at the picnic table, all of us as quiet as the morning. Nobody spoke. It was as if we were all holding our breath for news. Finally I heard the screen door of the farmhouse snap shut.

"Auntie Lynette's up," Alexis announced, and we both bounced out of our seats.

"Alex," Mr. Curry said, his voice a warning. "Give Kira a private moment with her family."

"But, Dad—"

"Let her go," he said. Alex reluctantly sat back down, leaving space for me to pass.

I ran to the farmhouse, my blanket flapping behind me like a cape. Halfway there I froze. What if it was bad news? What if it was something I didn't want to hear? Suddenly I felt like running away, but Mom had seen me.

"Kira!" she called from the veranda, waving, and we met on the lawn.

"Is it bad?" I asked. "Don't tell me if it's bad, okay?"

She kissed my forehead. "There's still a lot we don't know. She'll likely be in the hospital for a few more days. But she was sitting up in bed and barking orders when I left last night."

Up and talking. Barking orders. That had to be good, right? "So, she's going to be okay?" I asked.

"We don't know yet," Mom told me.

"But you said—"

Mom threw her arm over my shoulders. "I'm just saying that we don't have the whole picture yet."

I tightened the blanket around me, and we headed back to the bush camp.

Mr. Curry let Alexis and me head to the clinic before a proper breakfast, knowing that Mrs. Curry would need all the help she could get without Aunt Mamie. As we approached the clinic, we could see through the screen door that the wombats were running around. Boomer sprinted straight at us, colliding with the screen.

"You silly wombat," I said, slipping inside to scratch his bottom.

"Oh, great, girls—I'm glad you're here. Kira, can you feed Bean for me?" Mrs. Curry asked.

"Can I do it, Mum?" Alexis said. "I never get to feed him."

Her mother shook her head. "Bean has become attached to Kira, and he eats really well when she feeds him."

I blushed. "I'm sure he likes Alexis, too, Mrs. Curry—"

"You get to feed animals every day, Alex," her mom said, talking over me. "Kira's only here for a short stay, and anyway, I need help cleaning up the mess Boomer made in his box last night."

Alexis threw her hands up. "Mum! Are you kidding—"

Mrs. Curry put her hands on her hips. "Or you could catch up on schoolwork if you prefer."

They stared at each other until Alexis relented and stomped over to Boomer's box. The air felt thick with tension.

After feeding Bean I was hungry, so I went next door to the farmhouse kitchen. I found some leftover bacon and took it onto the veranda. I was hoping the cat would show up to keep me company, since Alex was still on cleanup duty. After checking for spiders under the cushions on the porch swing, I sat down, calling, "Here, kitty kitty kitty!"

Within a few minutes, the orange cat came out from the bush, tail twitching.

"Good morning," I whispered, patting the spot next to me on the swing. To my surprise, the cat hopped right up.

"Are you hungry?" I held out a piece of bacon, and the cat delicately took it and ate it.

The cat stayed with me on the swing, even after the bacon was gone. Very slowly, I put out my hand. The cat tensed up and looked as if it was about to run into the bush, but before it could zip away, I began to stroke the cat just above its tail, like I did with my foster kittens back home. Soon enough, I heard it: my new friend was purring.

FIELD STUDIES
Chapter 10

The following morning, there was still no new news about Aunt Mamie. After a quick breakfast, Alex and I went straight to the clinic, where things went much as they had the day before.

"You're on Bean duty, Kira. I need to dress the echidna's wound," Mrs. Curry said. "I've got the trainees tidying up the aviary. Boomer is outside in his pen. Blossom will need a bottle soon." She ticked things off on her fingers, talking to herself.

"What can I do?" Alexis asked, following her mom.

"The aquariums need cleaning, and Mum needs fresh eucalyptus branches. Don't give me that look, Alex," Mrs. Curry said.

"Mum!" Alex flung open her arms. "It's not fair. You keep giving me all the bad jobs!"

"Sweetheart," Mrs. Curry said calmly, "we all need to pitch in where we can while Aunt Mamie's in the hospital. And remember, your studies are your first priority. I'd like you to get caught up today. Kira may be on school holiday, but you are not."

I froze, about to sit in a rocking chair with Bean and a bottle when I heard my name. I tried not to make any noise while Mrs. Curry and Alexis faced off on the other side of the room. Bean grunted, ready to eat. Both of us jumped when Alexis slammed out the door.

I spent the rest of the morning in the clinic with Mrs. Curry and the trainees, preparing food, checking on Boomer in his outside pen with Muffin, and feeding Blossom her bottle. After that, I went to look for Alex, hoping to cheer her up. I found her in the farmhouse kitchen, surrounded by her schoolbooks.

"Hey," I said, pulling up a chair. "I've been thinking about something. You know how the other night . . ." I stopped talking because it was obvious Alex wasn't listening. "Are you all right?"

She crossed her arms. "I'm just mad, okay?"

"At me?" I asked.

"No." She picked at some chipping paint on the table. "Not really. I'm just frustrated."

Was it "no" or "not really"? Because those were two different things. "So, you are mad at me?" I asked again.

Alexis let out a sharp breath. "No, but I guess—it's like—well, I wish you stuck up for me a bit more. I've been doing all the bad jobs—cleaning up wombat poo and collecting leaves. And guess what, I don't like spiders either!"

She wouldn't look at me. "Aunt Mamie said I'd get to take care of the next joey, and now you're basically in charge of Bean."

It was like a punch to the gut. I mean, Alex lived here, where she could feed and play with and help raise joeys every day of her life, while I would soon be back home suffering through middle school. Without a best friend.

Before I could say anything, Mom and Auntie Lynette came into the kitchen.

"I was just coming to find you," Mom said to me. "Aunt Mamie really wants to see you today."

"We want to see her, too!" Alexis said, brightening. She closed the textbook she'd been reading.

"Oh," said Mom after an awkward pause. "Well, you're welcome to come with us if it's okay with your parents."

Alex looked down at her schoolwork, her cheeks pink. "That's okay," she said, and I wondered if she felt left out at not having been invited.

Auntie Lynette grabbed her keys. "Kira, ready to leave?"

My stomach tightened. The last time I had been in a hospital was after Dad's accident, and that was not a memory I wanted to relive. Besides, Alexis was still unhappy with me, and this was probably making it worse.

"Mom." I swallowed. My throat felt thick. "Can I stay here instead?"

"But Kira—" Mom started.

"Please?" I asked.

She shrugged. "Aunt Mamie will be disappointed. Are you sure?" I nodded, and she said, "Well, maybe next time." She kissed me on the forehead and left with Auntie Lynette.

When the door closed behind them, Alexis turned to me. "Why didn't you want to go?"

I shook my head, not sure how to explain it. Alexis waited, picking at the chipped paint again. I didn't want to tell her that I was scared. Of what I'd see at the hospital. Of Aunt Mamie being really sick. And also of making Alex even more mad at me if I went and she didn't.

Alexis cleared her throat, closing her notebook and lining up her pencils in perfect order. "Anyway, before this, you said you had something to tell me?"

"Yes!" I said, remembering why I had come to find her. "I had an idea for us." Suddenly I felt shy about telling her. "It's all right if you're not up for it, though."

"It depends on what it is," Alexis said.

"Okay, I think we should look for our bird again," I said. "The paradise parrot."

She looked at me impatiently. "Even though it's extinct?"

"Then how come we saw one?" I asked. "Come on, you heard what Evie said the other night. How you never know what you'll find in the bush." I leaned forward. "Like, maybe even a bird that's supposed to be extinct!"

Alexis rolled her eyes, but she opened her computer and began to type. "Okay, let's see if anyone has ever rediscovered an extinct animal in Australia before . . ." Her search results popped up, and she turned the laptop toward me. "Hey, it looks like they have. The crest-tailed mulgara, a tiny marsupial. Something called an Australian tree lobster—oh, wow, it's a huge bug, don't look."

The beetle-like creepy-crawly was easily as long as my forearm. I clapped my hands over my eyes.

"Told you!" she said, laughing, and I laughed, too.

"Hey, look," Alexis said, scrolling through another website. "It says here there's been a few sightings of the paradise parrot, actually. In Queensland." She read from the website: "While on holiday to Girraween National Park, a family of four witnessed what they believe to be a paradise parrot, a bird thought to be extinct since 1927, in a tree near their campsite. 'He was flying around like this!' their young son said, demonstrating how the bird flew. The sighting remains unconfirmed."

Alexis scrolled some more. "Looks like the other two sightings weren't proven either. But still . . ."

"Think about it," I said. "This is a big property—with plenty of termite mounds for the parrots to nest in." I held up my phone with the blurry photo I had taken of the bird.

"We just need to find our bird and get a better picture."

Alexis shook her head. "Do you know how many parrots are in the sanctuary? A bajillion. How could we ever find that bird again?"

"Maybe Shashi would let us borrow one of his song meters," I suggested. "We could see what kind of bird sounds we pick up. If one of them is the paradise parrot . . . Alex, just imagine if we found it!"

"We'd probably be on the news," Alexis said, finally warming up to the idea.

"And just think how excited Aunt Mamie and Auntie Lynette would be," I added. "Evie, too. Come on, what do we have to lose?"

Alexis gathered up her papers and books. "Let's go talk to Shashi about a song meter. I know exactly where we can put it."

Shashi was at the bush camp talking to Mr. Curry. I was prepared to wait patiently for a break in their conversation, but Alexis bounded right over, tugging on Shashi's shirt. "Can we please borrow a song meter?"

He broke into a grin. "You need a song meter? Are you going to help with my frog research?"

"It's for bird research," I explained.

Shashi rubbed his head. "I've got an old one you can use. It probably needs batteries. It's in the shed."

"Perfect!" Alexis and I said at the same time. "Thank you!" And we raced off.

When we got to the shed, Alexis opened the door and went inside as if she wasn't even worried about the spider webs all over. I paused in the doorway. "On a scale from one to ten, what are the chances there's a bunch of dangerous and deadly spiders in here?" I asked.

Alexis looked back at me. "Oh, I'd say there's a big chance. Probably an even bigger chance there's a snake or two." I shivered, but she pulled me inside. "I'll get the song meter, batteries, and zip ties. You get a stake for the ground." She pointed to a pile of metal stakes in a corner.

After building up some courage and rehearsing my escape to get help in case I got bitten by a venomous spider, I bravely walked in and grabbed a stake.

Once we had all our loot, we took the path behind the bush camp, crossing an open field and turning into the trees.

"Do you know where you're going?" I asked Alex. "I'd sure hate to get lost out here."

"It's just up ahead." After another five minutes of walking, she stopped in an area dotted with towers of dirt.

"Whoa," I said, looking around. "Are these termite mounds?"

They were huge—at least two feet wide and twice as high. One of them was up to my shoulders. I walked around and inspected the mounds for little bird-size dugouts like the ones I'd seen on the website showing how the parrots nested, but I didn't see any.

I was on my way back to Alexis, who was hammering the stake into the hard ground with a mallet, when I nearly stepped on a mouse. I bent down to examine it, recoiling when I realized it was only *part* of a mouse.

"Oh, no," I said. "This poor thing. Look."

Alexis came over and squatted in front of the little ball of fur. "Bugger. It's a pygmy possum. I reckon the predator got to it."

We worked faster then, aware that the predator could still be in the area. We inserted new batteries in the song meter, zip-tied it to the stake, flipped the switch on the bottom, and made sure the little red light went on so we knew it was working. Then we rushed back to the bush camp to tell Mrs. Curry about our gruesome find.

A CHANGE IN PLANS
Chapter 11

That evening, Mom and Auntie Lynette joined us at dinner after spending the day with Aunt Mamie. We ate barbecued chicken and potatoes and listened to Shashi talk about his latest frog discovery, a population of scarlet-sided pobblebonks. He even had a recording of their loud *bonk-bonk* frog calls on his song meter.

"It's hard to hear with all the other sounds and bird calls, but if you listen . . ." he held his ear for a moment and we all heard a faint *bonk-bonk*. "I'll be able to edit out the rest of the noise on my computer," he added.

"Can you show us how to do that, too?" I asked.

"Interested in frogs, are you?" Evie said, sitting across the table from Alexis and me.

"Actually, birds," Alexis said, her mouth full. "One bird in particular." We exchanged a look, but kept our paradise parrot research secret for now.

Evie lit up. "Birds, really? Well, let me know if you ever want to go out in the field with me. I'm watching a family of tawny frogmouths with two little fledglings. I think they're about to leave their nest any day now."

"I love tawny frogmouths," Alexis exclaimed.

"Then you'll love watching these," Evie said with a smile. She turned to me. "How much longer are you with us, Kira?"

"Only until Friday," I said, my excitement fizzling.

"Drat," she said. "Tomorrow I leave for university for a few days, so you'll be gone when I return. But I can take you out when I get back next weekend," she said to Alexis.

And the rest of my good mood officially left my body. Soon—too soon—I'd be on a plane, heading back to Michigan. I'd be buying school supplies instead of changing field batteries . . . searching for my locker instead of an extinct bird . . .

"Actually," Mom broke in, "there's been a change in our travel plans." Her face was serious. "Mamie has a heart condition, and it's a bit more complicated than we thought. Once she returns home, she'll have to take it easy for a while. So I've offered to extend our trip so that I can help look after Mamie while she recovers."

Everyone at the table was quiet now, listening.

"So, that means we're staying?" I asked, my heart pounding. "For how long?"

"Until the end of the summer," Mom said.

I had a thousand feelings all at once. Happy I'd get to stay at the sanctuary longer, but scared for Aunt Mamie's health. How long would it take for Aunt Mamie to feel better? When would she come home from the hospital? And who would run the vet clinic? I looked at Mom, not sure what to say. "I . . . I'm glad we're staying."

Mom gave me a hug. "I wish it could be for a different reason, too."

When Alexis and I went to the clinic the next morning, we found Mrs. Curry at the desk with a pile of paperwork.

"Alexis, do you mind taking the food out for the echidnas?" Her mother pointed to a tray on the table. "Then you can let Boomer and Daisy have some playtime in here while you clean their boxes." Daisy was the other young wombat who lived in the joey nursery with Boomer.

Alexis nodded and picked up the tray, which had holes in the lid that were sized just right for an echidna's pointy muzzle to slurp through. She went out to put it in Mum's pen, where the echidnas lived.

Mrs. Curry asked me to try feeding Bean. "He hasn't been eating well this morning. I need to peek in on stubborn old Dodger. We haven't fed him in days, but he still won't leave. He's going to end up back in the clinic if he's not careful." She got up and headed toward the door. "After Bean has had his meal, let's try him with Mum again, okay?"

"Sure," I said, lifting Bean out of his basket. But even when I snuggled with him in the rocking chair, he was too distracted to eat.

"Don't worry," I told him. "I won't let you fall out of the tree." I tried feeding him again, but the formula got all over his fur. I wiped it up and made a few more unsuccessful attempts before he finally settled in and took the bottle as I rocked him back and forth.

Alexis came back, fetched Boomer and Daisy from the nursery, and set them on the floor. Boomer immediately began running around acting silly, while Daisy tackled a stuffed animal. Alexis quickly cleaned their boxes and then came over to the rocking chair. "Can I take a turn?"

"Well," I whispered, "the thing is, he just started taking this bottle—"

Alex squinted at me. "I know how to feed a joey."

I looked down at Bean, still sucking his bottle and staring at me. "It's just that your mom said he hasn't been eating well," I explained.

She crossed her arms. "I've probably fed like one hundred fussy joeys in my life."

I hesitated. I could tell Alex was getting upset, but I also

knew that if I disturbed Bean, he'd stop drinking. And he
needed plenty of energy for his visit with Mum.

"We're supposed to be friends, Kira," Alexis went on,
officially losing patience with me. "Bean doesn't belong
to you." She stomped the tile foor, her face red, and Bean
reared away from his bottle, formula spurting everywhere.

"Alex, stop—you're scaring him!" I cried.

But she only got madder. "You're not the only one who
takes after Aunt Mamie, for your information!"

"Actually, I am!" I replied. Now *I* was mad. At her. For
startling Bean and interrupting his meal. For thinking she
knew how to take care of joeys better than I did. For claim-
ing my family as her own. "Aunt Mamie's not even your
real aunt!"

Alex gave me a wide-eyed look of shock and hurt, and
ran out of the clinic.

I took deep breaths, rocking Bean, hoping he'd settle
down and I could feed him some more, but my hands were
shaking. Thanks to Alexis's outburst, there was no way
Bean would eat now.

Mrs. Curry breezed into the clinic. "Let's get Bean out
there with Mum and see if today's the day she'll take him in
as one of her own—" She stopped. "Everything okay?"

I nodded and stood up with Bean, not wanting to talk
about it.

"A surrogate koala mother is the very best way to ensure Bean will be prepared for life in the wild," said Mrs. Curry.

Outside, the cool air calmed me down a bit. When we got to the koala enclosure, Mrs. Curry placed Bean on the branch near Mum. "Watch," she said, inching me back. "Let's see if he'll go to her himself."

Bean began climbing in Mum's direction as the big koala sat on the branch munching eucalyptus leaves. Then Bean stumbled, one of his back paws coming off the tree, and I stepped forward.

Mrs. Curry stopped me. "Let him be. He's learning."

But Bean had seen me. I tried tucking his teddy bear out of sight, but Bean cried, and I picked him up.

Mrs. Curry frowned. "Kira. He needs to bond with Mum; otherwise he'll end up back in the clinic, and his release schedule will be delayed."

"But he cried," I said. "Didn't you hear him? We can't let him cry like that; he's just a baby. Now he's happy. Look!" I positioned myself so she would see the little joey happily tucked in my arms.

Mrs. Curry sighed and said, "We'll try again tomorrow—and we'll leave the teddy inside."

The next day, the same thing happened. Bean cried as

soon as Mrs. Curry tried to take him from me, and he kept crying when she placed him on the branch by Mum.

Mrs. Curry sighed. "I don't think Bean is going to latch on to Mum if you're here, Kira."

"What?" I said, scratching Bean under the chin. "He'll be fine with me here. Watch." I positioned him on the branch myself, but when I stepped back he immediately started crying. My heart broke into a thousand pieces. But when I tried to pick him up, Mrs. Curry put her arm out to stop me.

"Go visit Boomer and Daisy. They're with Muffin in the outdoor wombat pen. It needs cleaning, so bring a rake with you."

I started to protest. "Maybe Bean's just not ready. He's still so little. And there's a predator on the loose! Don't they go after baby animals first?"

Mrs. Curry plucked the crying joey off the branch and soothed him. "This is part of animal rescue, Kira. We rehabilitate wild animals to release them. Bean belongs in the wild. You need to let go. It's hard, but if you don't, it could cost Bean the freedom he deserves."

She walked me to the gate. "You can visit him in the clinic, but I'm afraid you're not helping Bean by being here in the pen."

Stung, I walked very slowly out of Mum's pen, hoping

that Mrs. Curry would call me back, but she didn't.

In the wombat pen, Muffin was lying on her back by one of the tunnel entrances, sleeping. I peeked inside the hidey-holes and found Daisy and Boomer.

"Hey there, Boomer," I whispered. He perked up at my voice and came out to see me, shaking the sand off his fur. "Sorry, I don't have a carrot." I bent over to give him a scratch and then grabbed a rake to clean the pen, when I heard voices. Peering through the fence, I saw Mom and Auntie Lynette sitting at a picnic table by the shed.

"So you think we should plan for her retirement?" I heard Mom asking Auntie Lynette. "It doesn't sound like the doctor has much hope she can return to the clinic."

I froze. My heart hammered in my chest and I felt lightheaded. No hope Aunt Mamie could be a vet anymore? Because of her health?

"This community relies on us," Auntie Lynette replied. "We're the only wildlife clinic within an hour of here. We need a veterinarian on staff if we're going to continue to operate the sanctuary."

"Maybe the doctor is underestimating how well Mamie will recover," Mom said.

Auntie Lynette shook her head. "Maybe, but we can't assume that. We need to be prepared."

I waited for Mom to tell Auntie Lynette she was wrong.

To tell her that Aunt Mamie was strong and didn't give up, and she'd be back in that clinic like always just as soon as she got home. But Mom didn't say that. Instead she said, "I guess we should start looking to hire a replacement then."

A replacement? Nobody could replace Aunt Mamie!

It was all I could take. I dropped the rake and ran out of the enclosure, my feet pounding the hard, dry ground.

THE ESCAPE
Chapter 12

I knew where I could be alone: the greenhouse, a little shelter behind the clinic where eucalyptus branches were kept in tubs filled with water. As soon as I walked in, the smell of the fresh greens brought a tumble of memories. The last time we were here, it had been Dad's and my job to find the right kind of eucalyptus branches in the bush for the koalas to eat. We spent hours traipsing across the property, me with a walking stick to poke out any snakes that might be ahead of us, and Dad with some heavy-duty loppers.

I perched on an upside-down bucket and closed my eyes, soaking in the greenhouse smell, trying to capture every detail of how my dad looked back then. His favorite sun-bleached visor. His hiking boots with the bright red laces. The pack of spearmint gum in his pocket. I could see him as if he were here with me.

I tried to imagine what he would think about everything that was happening. About Aunt Mamie getting sick and maybe never working in the clinic again. I bet he'd say that Aunt Mamie was tough and didn't give up that easily. I bet he'd never in a million years rush off and hire a new veterinarian to replace her.

Suddenly my thoughts were interrupted by a shout. "The wombats!" It was Mrs. Curry, and she sounded panicked. I ran out of the greenhouse so fast, I almost tripped over my own feet. "Get the nets!" she yelled. "The wombats are loose!"

A terrible, tingling feeling buzzed through my body. I had been the last person in their enclosure. I had left in such a rush. Had I forgotten to lock the door behind me?

"We have more big nets in the shed," Auntie Lynette called.

Mom, Shashi, and Evie joined the search. Mr. Curry's drone blinked past me, and I saw Alex bolt up the hill with a net, but I could only stand there, frozen, feeling mortified and ashamed. This was all my fault. I wanted to zip myself into my tent until it was over.

"Reckon this is not a time for standing still, dear." It was Auntie Lynette, hooking my elbow and steering me to the open area between the wombat enclosure and the shed. "We've got an emergency, otherwise known as a *do-something situation*."

We slowed down, passing the parrots and the possums. "There!" she whispered, pointing to a tubby brown animal nosing around a wheelbarrow. "Got Muffin over here!" she called over her shoulder, then murmured to me, "They don't like going too far from their food source, that's for sure."

One of the student trainees swooped by with a giant net. "Got her!"

One down, two wombats to go. We looked all over the shed and the open area, but found no more wombats on the loose. Finally we set off down a path that led into the more wild part of the sanctuary.

As we hiked I looked around, half hoping to spot Alexis. She had a way with wombats, and if anyone could find them, she could. But I didn't see her, and after an hour of searching, we came up empty-handed. I slumped down on a rock. My face was red and sweating, and I felt like crying.

"Have some water," Auntie Lynette said, handing me a canteen.

Even though I was hot and thirsty, it was hard to swallow past the lump in my throat, because all I could think of were Daisy and Boomer. If anything were to happen to them, it would be all my fault. Alexis would never forgive me. Where was she, anyway?

Suddenly I heard shouts, and Mr. Curry appeared through the trees, calling, "We found Daisy!" He was looking down at his tablet, streaming live video from his drone. "She's up ahead, by the perimeter fence." He pointed and we started fast in that direction, just as Alex came running down the path, passing him in her hurry to reach Daisy.

"Don't scare her," Mr. Curry called. "Wombats are fast little buggers when they're scared. We could be chasing her all night."

Suddenly we heard a loud and terrifying cry. I knew right away it was the sound of an animal in pain. And then everyone was tearing ahead toward Daisy—except for me. I was too afraid of what I'd find when I reached the fence. Straggling behind, I heard more commotion and shouting and Auntie Lynette calling for help. And then in the middle of it all, I heard a different sound: the undeniable scream of an animal—but it didn't sound like a wombat.

"Get that cat!" Mr. Curry yelled from the fence as Alexis and Auntie Lynette took off with their nets.

Cat? That shook me out of my stupor.

"Wait!" I called. "Is he striped orange with green eyes? Because I know that cat. He's gentle. He'd never attack a wombat."

Alexis stopped in her tracks and spoke to me for the first time that day. "What do you mean, you know that cat?"

"Sometimes we hang out in the mornings. He—he likes bacon," I stammered. By the look on Alexis's face, this was not the right answer.

"That gentle cat happens to be the predator we've been looking for! How did you not know that?" Alexis bit off the words and spat them at my feet.

"I—just . . ." I faltered. I knew cats were predators, but—
"I thought we were looking for a fox! It's just a cat!"

"It's not *just* a cat. It's a *feral* cat, and they're killing
everything in Australia!" Alexis shouted.

"Cats?" I couldn't believe it.

"Yes. Cats," she said, giving me a withering look.
"They've killed so many of our native animals that some
have even gone extinct. Ever heard of the rusty numbat?"

"Um, no," I said.

"Exactly. Because feral cats have killed them all."

"Oh," I said quietly. "I had no idea."

"Got Daisy!" called Auntie Lynette.

Alexis and I turned to see the squirming wombat
pinned under her net. Mr. Curry popped a gunnysack
over Daisy and picked her up, still in the sack, and we all
trudged back to the clinic carrying our nets and one injured
wombat.

That left Boomer still on the loose. Along with the cat.

That night it took me a long time to fall asleep. I couldn't
stop thinking about Daisy back in the clinic, all scratched
up and frightened from her encounter with the cat. But what
really kept me awake was worrying about Boomer. Out in

the bush, in the dark. For a hungry predator on the prowl, a baby wombat would be a perfect target. I felt sick thinking about it.

When I heard the zipper on the tent open, I sat bolt upright in bed, spooked. But it wasn't a rabid predator trying to get into the tent. It was just Alexis, leaving.

"Where are you going?" I asked.

"To the bathroom," she said.

"In your muck boots?"

She looked at her boots. "Okay, I'm going to find Boomer."

"What? Now?" I staggered out of bed. "You can't. It's the middle of the night!"

"I know," she whispered. "But I can't leave Boomer out there helpless by himself."

"No way," I said, stepping closer to her. I remembered the stern lecture from Aunt Mamie on my first night here: *There is a rule here on the property: no nighttime bush walks without an adult. Understand?*

"It's not safe," I reminded her. "And it's against the rules."

Alexis snorted. "I knew you'd say that. Everyone goes on and on about how much you take after Aunt Mamie and have a special connection with animals and blah, blah, blah. But they're wrong. You're nothing like her. Aunt Mamie would never forget to close a gate. She would never feed a feral cat. And now Boomer could get killed tonight. But I'm not going to let that happen." She turned and walked out of the tent.

I stumbled back at her words, but I couldn't let her just leave. I stuffed my feet into my shoes and dashed after her. "Alex!"

"Shhh!" she said, whirling around. "Just let me go, Kira."

"I can't let you go out there alone!"

"You know, I take back what I said about your friend in Michigan. How she was wrong for telling you to go with the flow. She was right." Alexis pointed at me, and it felt like a dagger to my heart. "You try to control everything, and that is the worst kind of friend."

She didn't even let me respond, just marched out of camp and onto the path. I ran after her. I didn't have a flashlight and the air was chilly without a sweatshirt, but Alexis was getting away and who knew how many dangerous things were out there? There was no time to go back, and I couldn't just let her walk off into the Australian wilderness alone. I had to stop her.

Alexis barreled out of the bush camp and past the pens and clinic and shed, setting off on the path into the woods. It was the same path we'd taken the day we installed our song meter. I followed her, calling, "Alex! Wait!"

By the time I made it to the termite mounds, I couldn't

see her. "Alex, I don't have a flashlight! Come back!" I yelled, my voice swallowed up by the darkness.

I saw the beam of her flashlight off to my right and followed it. The trees were closer together and the ground more uneven, throwing me off balance. I glimpsed Alexis one more time, her white sweatshirt through the trees, before she vanished into the forest.

Knowing it would be useless to try to follow her, I turned back, searching for the termite mounds, which should have been straight behind me a few yards away. But they weren't. I blinked in the dark, turning slowly in a circle. No termite mounds. No path. I had walked farther than I thought.

I was lost and alone, without a flashlight, in the middle of the Australian bush.

LOST

Chapter 13

The darkness was a kind of dark I had never experienced before. Darker than my room at home with my blackout shades. Darker than taking a walk on a moonless night. A complete and total darkness. But it wasn't silent. The darkness thrummed with life. Chirps and grunts and flaps. Little feet skittering on dry leaves all around me.

All the time I'd spent preparing for danger, planning so I'd be safe, and here I was with no light to help me find a path back home and the temperature dropping with no way to keep warm. I had failed to stop Alexis, or even to help her.

Alexis was right. I was nothing like Aunt Mamie. I had ruined Bean's chances of bonding with Mum. I had left the wombat pen open. I had befriended a predator and put the whole sanctuary at risk.

Alexis was right—I wasn't cut out for animal rescue. I couldn't even rescue myself.

"Helloooooo!" I yelled. How far was I from camp? Was there a chance someone could hear me? *Heeellllp!* I tried again, my voice fading into the tall trees as a feeling of dread settled in my chest.

I felt something crawling on my bare arm. I flapped it off and heard it scurry away. My entire body broke out in goose bumps. Feeling like there were things crawling on me, I began frantically brushing off my arms and shoulders and face and neck, barely holding back a total freak-out.

I can't stay here, I can't stay here, I thought to myself. Not without a light or bug spray or even a sweatshirt. I had no choice but to look for the trail. If I could just find the termite mounds, maybe I could find my way back.

I took three steps and my foot landed on something soft. I lost my balance, pitching forward, trying not to fall on whatever creature I had just stepped on. I heard a loud hiss as the creature fled, leaving me alone once again, my heart beating out of my chest.

I stood up, maniacally brushing myself off, wondering how many spiders and beetles and snakes were in the leaves. Afraid to stand still and afraid to walk anywhere, I danced in place frantically, fighting down panic.

After what felt like an hour, I saw a flash of light between the trees. "Alex?" I shrieked. "Alex, is that you?" I froze, whispering *please-please-please-please*, my eyes closed—or maybe open, it was too dark to tell. And then I saw the light again and screamed louder. *"Hello! Alex? Please be there!"*

I heard a faint response—"Kira!" And then louder,

"Kira, is that you?"

"I'm here!" I yelled back, nearly sobbing with relief. "I'm right here! Follow my voice!"

"Where?" She sounded scared. "I can't find you!"

And then, all of a sudden, there was movement in a nearby bush and I braced myself for whatever might jump out, relieved beyond words when it was Alexis, carrying a flashlight.

We ran to each other and hugged, afraid to let go. "I've been looking all over for you!" she cried. "I'm so sorry I kept going like that—"

"I was calling your name and—"

"—What was I even thinking?" Alexis said, both of us talking at the same time. "And now we're out here—"

"—It's okay," I said. "We just need to stick together."

"Are you freezing?" she asked, noticing I didn't have a sweatshirt.

"Not yet." My frantic dancing had kept me warm, but now I could feel the sweat turning cold and clammy on my skin. "Do you know where we are?" I asked. "How do we get out of here?"

"I'm not sure. I must have taken a wrong turn." She shined her light around. We saw nothing, but we heard rustling and skittering everywhere. Creatures were all around us, and it was clear we were the intruders in this scenario.

"Maybe they're looking for us by now," I said. "We could send a signal. Do you know how to start a fire?"

"No fires," Alexis said. "Way too much dry litter here. We'd start a bushfire."

"Right," I said. "Okay, bad idea." I seemed to be full of them.

Alexis sat down on a rock, which was very brave considering the number of creepy-crawlies that probably called that rock home.

"Do you think if we aimed your light straight up into the trees, someone might see it?" I asked.

"No, because they probably don't even know we're missing. Besides, we need to conserve the battery." Alexis shut the flashlight off but a second later flicked it on, shining it where a lizard was crawling near her knee. She leaped up and brushed herself off, then turned off the flashlight. "We'll never find Boomer in the dark. He might even have gone into a burrow underground. Let's just stay here until it's light, and then maybe we can find our way home before anyone notices that we're gone."

We stayed that way for a long time, just standing there in the dark. Finally Alex said, "Hey. I . . . um . . . I'm really sorry about everything I said back there. I didn't mean it—"

I stopped her. "You were right. I'm not anything like Aunt Mamie. It's my fault Daisy got hurt. I've put Boomer,

Bean, and the whole sanctuary at risk."

"We all make mistakes," Alexis said. "I mean, hunting for a wombat in the middle of the night wasn't my most brilliant idea," she snorted. "Don't be so hard on yourself. I know you like to be prepared, but sometimes things just happen."

"Yeah." She was right about that, too. "I feel—I don't know—safer when I research and plan ahead, as if I can prevent something bad from happening. But I guess it doesn't always work."

"Well, you know what Aunt Mamie says, right?"

I looked at her. "You can't let fear of the worst keep you from living your best."

"That's right."

"Yeah." I sighed. "She probably thinks I need to go with the flow, too."

"I'm sorry for saying you were too controlling," said Alexis. "It was mean of me to say, and mean of your best friend, too." She hopped a bit to stay warm, and then asked, "Do you think you'll ever be friends with her again?"

"We don't like the same things anymore," I said. "She's all the way into soccer, and I just want to hang out with the kittens at the shelter. She doesn't even like cats."

"Well, that makes two of us," Alexis said with a chuckle. Then she added, "Maybe you're just growing apart. You

could still be friends—just maybe not in the same way."

"Maybe," I agreed. "Still, it feels like giving up on a friendship, and I don't like giving up on things."

"Is it giving up?" Alexis asked. "Or letting go?"

I thought about that. Letting go of a rescue animal when it was ready meant giving it a new chance at life in the wild. You had to know when it was time to let go, so you weren't holding it back. Maybe it was the same for my friendship with Laila. "You know, Alex, you're pretty smart." I bonked her with my shoulder.

"That's really nice of you to say in this current situation." She linked her arm with mine.

I smiled, remembering where we were and why. "Seriously, I'm sorry for not standing up for you earlier. It wasn't fair for me to hog Bean like that."

"No, Kira." She turned the flashlight back on. "I was the one being a dag. My mum is right. You're the guest and you should experience everything. I can feed a koala joey another time."

"You're so lucky you get to live here," I said.

"Well, you know what?" she said. "I wish Mamie and Lynette *were* my aunts. My *real* aunts."

Shame burned my cheeks. "Alex, I should never have said that. You're all a family here. I was jealous."

She leaned her head on my shoulder. "We're jealous of

each other. Maybe it's because we have so much in common."

We stayed like that for a few minutes, standing close to keep warm, when there was a piercing cry that made us jump out of our skin.

"Peacock!" we said together.

"Hey, what's a dag, anyway?" I asked, when my heart stopped racing.

"Officially? Poo stuck in the wool of a sheep." She giggled. "Definitely my favorite insult."

We stopped talking for a while. Every so often Alexis turned on her flashlight to make sure we were safe from bugs and beetles and snakes. It was cold, and I began shivering out of control. I pictured my bed in the tent, with my warm sleeping bag. I pictured cuddling little Bean.

All at once, I heard a buzzing sound. It grew louder and closer. I grabbed Alexis's arm. Killer bees? Mosquitoes on a mission? Vampire bats? Anything could happen out here . . .

Suddenly, there was a bright spotlight moving through the trees. We looked up and saw Mr. Curry's drone flying slowly over us. We waved at the blinking camera, immensely relieved to be found—but also realizing we were totally busted.

CONSEQUENCES
Chapter 14

A untie Lynette woke us up early the next morning. "He's back," she said, sitting on the end of my cot.

I sprang up. "Boomer?"

Auntie Lynette nodded.

"Alexis!" I called, and she poked her head out of her covers. "Boomer's back!"

She flipped herself upright. "Is he okay?"

"He has a cut over his eye that needed a couple of stitches," Auntie Lynette said. "Found him munching on carrot peels in the wheelbarrow by the shed at sunrise. He's a little dirty but seems downright pleased with his night-time romp, if you ask me."

Alex grinned. "Can we see him?"

"Nope," she said. "Got something else in mind for you two." And then she rustled us out of our nice warm beds, not even caring that we needed extra sleep after our all-night adventure in the bush.

"Hey, I'm doing you two a favor," she said as she marched us up the path toward the farmhouse. "You should have heard some of the punishments your mothers were talking about. Scraping cockatoo poo off the veranda, cleaning all the loos, being banned from the animal clinic, doing the dishes for the rest of your lives . . ." Alexis and I groaned. "Something to think about next time you're tempted to go into the bush at night," she said sharply.

At the driveway, Auntie Lynette led us to a huge pile of shredded bark as high as my waist. "Just received our mulch delivery," she announced, "and I decided not to pay the extra fifty dollars to have it spread around the gardens." She clapped our shoulders. "Not when I have two strong young sheilas here to do the job."

"We have to do this all by ourselves?" I asked.

"It was only fifty dollars?" Alexis said.

"Hey, fifty dollars can get me a nice pedicure while I wait for you to finish the job," she said, producing two pitchforks.

"You don't get pedicures," I said dryly.

She handed us each a pitchfork, pointed at the wheelbarrows sitting in the driveway, and, with a wave, left us.

"Can't we have breakfast first?" I asked in a small voice, but my aunt didn't seem to hear.

"This is child abuse!" Alex called after her, but it was no use.

We worked for three hours. Three hours of hard, sweaty labor. Mom and Mrs. Curry stopped by more than once to

lecture us on following the rules and what were we thinking and we could've been seriously hurt out there. When
Mr. Curry visited, he handed us each a brekky sausage roll
he'd snuck out of the bush kitchen. We even had a few emus
and kangaroos check in to see what we were doing before
we finally reached the bottom of the mulch mountain.

"Want to check on Boomer and Daisy after this?" Alexis
asked, scraping the last of the mulch off the driveway with
a rake.

"No." I started pushing my wheelbarrow down to the
shed. "I can't face your mom after the mess I made of things
yesterday."

Alexis followed me. "Kira, you're not the only one who
messed up. Besides, you can't stay away from the clinic for
the rest of your time here."

I parked the wheelbarrow in the shed. "Yes, I can," I told
her. "You can feed Bean from now on."

Alex took a firm hold of my arm and began steering me
toward the clinic. "That's it, we're going *now*. Together."

I didn't know who I dreaded seeing more, Mrs. Curry
or Boomer with stitches over his eye or Daisy with injuries
from the predator. Alexis pushed me inside the clinic.

"Good afternoon, girls," Mrs. Curry said, standing over
the pygmy possum's aquarium. "Are you both sufficiently
sorry for your reckless behavior last night?"

CONSEQUENCES

We nodded emphatically.

"How is Daisy?" Alexis asked, and Mrs. Curry led us to a large pen in the corner of the clinic where the wombat was sleeping, paws up, on her back, in a pile of blankets.

"She's got some scratches and puncture wounds," said Mrs. Curry, "and she's missing a bit of fur on her backside, but that's expected, since wombats use their bums to defend themselves."

"What?" I asked.

"Wombats have a bony bum," Alexis explained. "It's tough enough to be used as a deadly weapon if they're attacked."

"Their butt is a deadly weapon?" I asked, and we both started giggling hysterically.

But then we got serious again, following Mrs. Curry to Boomer's old wooden box in the joey nursery. "If a predator gets into a wombat's burrow, the wombat can crush it with his bum," she told me, pulling Boomer out of his box and snuggling him into the crook of her arm.

"Whoa," I said, looking at Boomer with new appreciation.

"Can I hold him?" Alexis took the woozy wombat to the rocking chair while I lingered in the kitchen area, feeling guilty all over again. Normally Boomer would be dashing around the clinic, bumping into things, and tearing things apart, but he was so quiet.

"Is Boomer going to be okay?" I asked.

"He's just knackered from the painkillers," Mrs. Curry said from the sink. "Don't worry, he'll perk up."

"Does he have to stay in the clinic long?" I asked.

She shrugged. "At least a few days. Maybe a week to fully heal. We don't want to risk an infection."

I slumped. "That's a long time." I patted Boomer gently on the head. "I'm so sorry I let you out, buddy."

"Stop it," Alexis said. "Nobody's mad at you."

Boomer opened his eyes for a minute and looked at us before drifting back off to sleep. It felt as if he were saying, *I forgive you. Now be quiet and let me sleep!*

A moment later, Mrs. Curry came over and handed me a blanket-wrapped bundle. "I thought you might want to see him."

"My little Bean," I said, melting. He was asleep. "Is he okay? Has he bonded with Mum yet?"

Mrs. Curry exhaled. "Things aren't going so well with that. It's clear that Bean is not going to bond with Mum."

I stroked him between his ears. "What can we do?"

"There's a koala sanctuary a few hours from here, and they have a mother koala who just lost her baby, so we're thinking—"

"You're sending Bean away?" My voice caught in my throat.

CONSEQUENCES

Mrs. Curry put her hand on my arm. "I know it's not what we were hoping. But we need to do what's best for Bean."

"Are you sure leaving here is best for him?" I blinked hard, trying not to cry. Bean was awake now, hugging his teddy bear.

"Yes, dear," Mrs. Curry said softly.

I rubbed Bean under his neck, sniffling. "Does he have to leave soon?"

"Day after tomorrow," Mrs. Curry said.

Bean looked up at me with his dark eyes and I hugged him, never wanting to let go.

THE VISIT

Chapter 15

Mom was just about to get in the car when I caught her. "Wait!" I called.

She turned around. "You want to come with me to visit Aunt Mamie?"

It wasn't exactly that I *wanted* to go; it was more that I couldn't stop thinking about what Auntie Lynette had said to me when the wombats got out. Although I was worried about seeing Aunt Mamie in the hospital, this was not a time to run away from my worries. It was a do-something situation. And I knew what I had to do.

The forty-minute drive went too fast, and before I knew it, we had arrived at the hospital. Mom held my hand as we walked into the big building and took the elevator to the fifth floor, where nurses bustled around and a patient pushed a walker down the hall. I swallowed. The chemical odor of strong cleaner mixed with whatever they served for lunch brought me back to Dad's time in the hospital. It was one of my last memories of him, that hospital smell.

Mom patted my hand. "You okay?"

I felt slightly sick to my stomach, but I pressed on. "I'm

okay." I repeated those words in my head as we walked into Aunt Mamie's room.

"There's my favorite wallaby!" Aunt Mamie said from the bed, reaching out to me.

Mom gave me a little push, and I walked over to my great-aunt, feeling the tightness in my throat loosen. The room was bright and sunny, and her favorite show about people buying houses was playing on the TV. She didn't look pale or sickly. She looked like regular old Aunt Mamie. Relief flooded through me as I hugged her. Then she patted the chair next to her bed for me to sit.

"Darling?" she said to Mom. "I feel thoroughly deprived of caffeine. Would you mind?"

Mom smiled. "I'll go get you a coffee, Mamie."

When Mom left, Aunt Mamie turned to me. "How is the sanctuary? Tell me everything. What did Mr. Curry make for dinner last night?"

"Uh, I think it was barramundi on the barbecue," I told her.

"One of my favorites. And straight off the barbie? Delectable." She took a sip of her water. "What's wrong, dear? Not a fan of fish?"

"Aunt Mamie." I got straight to the point. "I don't want Bean to go away." I looked down at my hands.

She put her glass down. "My dear bunny, I know this is hard. You and Bean have a strong connection."

"It's my fault he has to leave," I told her, blinking fast to stop the tears.

Aunt Mamie lifted my chin. "There is a balance while taking care of animals that is learned through experience. Without you, Bean might not have started taking his meals. He wouldn't have gained all the weight he did. Without you, he wouldn't be ready to begin transitioning to life in the wild. The balance is knowing when to step back and when to let go. Letting go is the only way to give a wild animal the freedom it needs."

I sniffed, wiping my eyes. Aunt Mamie handed me a tissue. "I always thought I was good at knowing what animals needed," I said, blotting my cheeks with the tissue. "But I've been messing up so much lately."

"You're too hard on yourself, dear."

"Aunt Mamie, I let the wombats out. I mean it was an accident, but then Daisy got attacked by a cat that I thought was harmless, and Boomer went on a midnight romp and got injured." I sucked in some air. "And now, thanks to me, they're both in the clinic again. Back where they started."

"And you know what?" Aunt Mamie said. "They'll heal right up, and I bet Boomer and Daisy have already forgiven you." She patted my hand. "And I might suggest you do the same. No time for pity parties around here." She looked at me sternly, and I flushed.

"I'm just . . . I'm not as tough as you," I faltered.

"Release days are difficult, even for this old lady," she went on. "But necessary—to give an animal its life back and to make room at the sanctuary for other animals in need."

She smiled. "Don't be fooled by my tough old hide. With every animal we release goes a piece of my heart."

I wiped my eyes again, wondering if Aunt Mamie ever felt as if she were giving away her *whole* heart. "Can Bean at least stay until after I return to Michigan at the end of the summer? So I don't have to see him go?"

"You can't avoid the things in life that are upsetting," Aunt Mamie said gently. "When I turned the ripe age of seventy, I just sort of realized how much easier it is to face difficult things straight on. The car with the shot brakes? Took it right in and got it fixed. Toothache? Called the dentist right up."

I wasn't buying it. "It would be easier for both of us— for Bean and me—if you just waited until after I leave."

"But it wouldn't be best for Bean," said Aunt Mamie. "The sooner he leaves the clinic and bonds with a foster mum, the better off he'll be." She reached up and stroked my hair.

"Here's how I face these hard moments: I remind myself of the things in life that bring me joy. Like beautiful birds. Ice cream with peanuts. Warm campfires on a dark night. A warm drink on a cold morning."

I gave her a skeptical look, but she was undeterred.

"Now you try it," she urged. "Think of something you enjoy, something good in your life."

I thought of Alexis's friendship, Bean slurping his formula, and watching the sunrise on the veranda. I didn't feel an instant relief, but I did feel a flutter in my chest, a loosening in my shoulders. "You promise they'll take good care of him?" I asked, blowing my nose.

She crossed her heart. "I swear on this applesauce." She picked up a covered bowl. "Do you want this, by the way?" I shook my head. "How about ice chips?" she asked. "They have a machine that makes them. Best ice chips for crunching when you're bored."

"No thanks." I couldn't think about applesauce or ice chips at a time like this.

"Rehabilitating wild animals is not for the faint of heart. But you are tough, Kira. I know you can do this."

She checked her watch and then took the remote from her bedside table and began scrolling through the channels.

"Aunt Mamie?"

"Yes?" she said, not looking away from the TV.

"I'm really sorry I didn't come to see you earlier."

She waved me off. "It's okay, my pet. You're here now."

"You're coming home tomorrow, right?" I said.

"I believe so. But, dear, there will be some changes when I get back," she said, putting a hand on her chest. "Your old Mamie's heart is not what it used to be."

"On a scale from one to ten, how bad is it?" I tried to sound calm.

She turned to face me. "I have heart disease. That means I can't work at the clinic for a while. I'll have to ask for help more often. Maybe we'll have to hire another vet."

I had already heard this from Auntie Lynette, but hearing it from Mamie herself felt like a dodge ball to the gut.

"I will miss being as active as I used to be," she added, "but if I take care of myself, I should have years left with this heart."

I took a breath. Chocolate cookies on a long flight. Being with Alexis on a dark night. Bottle-feeding a cuddly joey.

Aunt Mamie pushed a strand of hair out of my face. "I have plenty of reasons to feel grateful— and one of them is sitting right here." She reached over and pulled me into a hug, and then we watched people buy beach houses on TV while we ate applesauce and ice chips.

DISCOVERY
Chapter 16

The next day Alexis and I headed over to the farm-house right after breakfast so that we could be there when Mom brought Aunt Mamie home.

Auntie Lynette was on the phone. She put a finger to her lips when she saw us. "Did you say October?"

"Who is she talking to?" Alexis whispered. I shrugged.

Auntie Lynette went on. "No, right . . . yes, I understand that but—" And then, a minute later, "Sure. No worries. Thank you." She hung up, and then stood in front of us, her arms folded. "And may I ask what you two are doing here when I'm trying to have an important conversation with the chief of the rural fire brigade?"

"Waiting for Aunt Mamie?" I offered.

"Mamie won't be here for hours, so you'd best find something to do before I find it for you. We've got quite a lot of loos around here that need cleaning."

We hopped up at her threat, heading for the door. "Why were you talking to the fire chief?" I asked.

Auntie Lynette opened the front door. "I'd like to have some fireys come and look at our property. I need advice on extra precautions we can take to keep our animals safe if there's a bushfire."

"But summer hasn't even started," said Alexis.

"Doesn't matter anymore, pumpkin. Remember last winter? Thanks to climate change and drought, fire season is now year-round." Auntie Lynette's phone rang. "I've got to take this." She pushed us out the door. "Find something useful to do."

"Let's go see what got recorded on our song meter," I suggested.

"Great idea!" said Alex.

So we followed the trail to the termite mounds to retrieve the song meter and then took it back to the clinic to use the computer.

When Alexis sat down at the workstation, Boomer skidded over to investigate. I was glad to see he was feeling better. Alexis plugged the song meter into the computer, downloaded the audio file, and imported it into the program that would analyze it. Boomer pulled a tissue out of a tissue box, shaking his head and galloping around with it.

"Ready?" Alexis hovered her finger over the button to start the analysis.

I gave her a thumbs-up. "Let's do it!"

And science was amazing, because in about three

seconds the program was finished and we had a ton of little files to sort through. Alexis clicked on the first one.

"Oh, wow!" I said as a graph popped up with a green line going up and down in a pattern of peaks and valleys.

"It's a picture of the birdsong," Alexis said. "Cool."

She clicked on the next one. Each bird call recorded on the song meter had been turned into a similar picture. Alexis said the pictures were called *spectrograms* and that each one was unique to the bird that had made the sound.

I pointed to an option on the computer program labeled "Auto Identify" and asked, "Should we try that?"

"Good idea," said Alexis. A second later, our files were organized into folders labeled with the bird that went with each birdsong: kookaburra, black cockatoo . . . "Whoa. A black cockatoo?" Alexis said. "Those are kind of rare around here!"

Currawong, red wattlebird, wonga pigeon . . . The more bird names I read that weren't the paradise parrot, the more disappointed I felt. Finally we reached the end of the list.

"There's a folder called 'Unknown,'" Alex said, clicking on it. "Looks like there's only one file in it."

"So there's one birdsong that the program couldn't identify?" I asked, pushing Boomer away from my shoelaces.

Alexis raised her eyebrows. "Maybe because it's from a bird that's supposed to be extinct."

DISCOVERY

We looked at each other for a moment. Then Alexis printed out the unknown spectrogram and grabbed my hand. "Let's find Evie and see if she knows what kind of bird made this song."

On our way to the bush camp, we ran into Alexis's dad, who was fiddling with an animal trap. It looked like a cage with a slanted door. I'd seen them before at the cat shelter back home.

He stood up and sighed. "Little bugger's too smart to be trapped."

"Are you trying to catch the cat?" I asked.

Mr. Curry nodded. "Reckon he'll not be an easy one to catch. Got any ideas, cat lady?"

"Try putting some of your breakfast sausage in there, or bacon. He likes those," I said, blushing.

"Dad," Alexis interrupted, "we're in a bit of a rush to see Evie. D'you know where she's at?"

"Probably out in the field, possum. She usually stays out all day."

Alexis frowned. "We have something *really* important—"

Suddenly we heard a car door slam, which meant Aunt Mamie was home from the hospital! Alexis and I ran to the farmhouse to greet her.

When we got there, Auntie Lynette was trying to get Aunt Mamie to use a walker on the uneven sidewalk beside the farmhouse, but Mamie was having none of it.

"Crikey, Mamie, you'll bust a hip before we even get you inside!" Auntie Lynette exclaimed.

"Do I look like an old lady?" Aunt Mamie muttered back, but she reached for Auntie Lynette's hand, giving it a kiss, and allowed Lynette to guide her up the stairs to the veranda.

I was relieved to have my great-aunt back, but I knew that even though she was home and acting like her regular self, her heart was not fixed. No amount of research or preparation would cure it. No tools or precautions would change her diagnosis. It was just a reality we'd have to deal with from now on.

Aunt Mamie sat in a rocking chair, and Mom brought out tea and cookies. A few emus wandered by, sticking their beaks through the rails on the veranda, and Auntie Lynette shooed them away with her napkin.

"So," Aunt Mamie said, getting comfortable in her chair with her tea and a Tim Tam, "what have I missed?"

"Well, the rural fire brigade is coming to look at our property," Auntie Lynette said. "They'll give us some tips to reduce the risk of a bushfire. And as you can see, our mulch delivery came—" but before she could say any more, we saw Evie walking up the path with her gear.

"Hello there, dear," Aunt Mamie called to her. "Come

have yourself some tea. You've been working hard, I'm sure."

"G'day," Evie called back. "Happy to see you home, Mamie." She peeled off her backpack and stepped onto the veranda.

Alex and I nudged each other, each trying to push the other to say something to her. When Evie made eye contact with me, I cleared my throat. "Um, Evie?" I suddenly felt shy to be bothering a scientist with our idea, because what if she thought it was dumb?

That didn't stop Alex from barging ahead. "Kira and I have a question for you."

"Shoot," Evie said, taking a Tim Tam.

Alex took the printout of the spectrogram from her pocket and unfolded it on the table.

"It's a spectrogram," I said, then felt silly because of course Evie would know what it was. "We recorded it near the termite mounds," I added, in case it was helpful information. I was about to add, "That's where paradise parrots like to nest," when Aunt Mamie broke in.

"You two collected and analyzed this data by yourselves?" Aunt Mamie put a hand to her heart. "I've never been so proud! What sort of bird did you find?"

"Well," I began, "the computer program knew all the sounds we recorded—" I looked at Alexis, and we both said, "except for one," at the same time.

"So Evie, we were wondering if you thought maybe it could be from—from a paradise parrot," I blurted, suddenly feeling ridiculous.

Auntie Lynette nearly choked on her Tim Tam. "Did you say paradise parrot?"

I nodded. "When we were out in the bush the other day, Alex and I saw this bird. It was blue and green, with black and red wings and a bit of red on the shoulder. Alex said she'd never seen one like it. I tried to take a picture, but it flew away."

"And then when we got back, Kira found it in my bird guide," Alexis chimed in. "The book said the parrot's extinct, but we know what we saw, and that bird looked just like the picture of the paradise parrot in my book."

Auntie Lynette glanced at Aunt Mamie. "That's very interesting. Because about five years ago, Mamie and I thought we spotted a paradise parrot."

"What?" Evie said, looking up from the spectrogram.

"You did?" Alexis and I said at the same time.

"How did I not know this?" Evie said, standing up. "Why did nobody tell the bird lady about a possible paradise parrot sighting on the property?"

"We spent a lot of time looking for it," Aunt Mamie said, "but we never saw it again, so we figured we were mistaken."

DISCOVERY

Evie reached into her bag and pulled out a binder. "I've never seen this spectrogram before." She leafed through pages and pages of spectrograms. "I keep every one I record, and I memorize them so that in the field I can identify birds faster. But this one . . . this one is different."

My pulse quickened. Was it possible? Could Alex and I have found an extinct bird?

"Here's the picture I took." I handed them my phone with the photo on my screen. "It's pretty blurry, but you can see the colors."

"Crikey," Auntie Lynette said, taking my phone and showing the photo to Aunt Mamie. "Look at those colors. A lot like that bird we saw five years ago."

Evie squinted at the photo on my phone. "Wow. Can you send me the song file and that photo?"

"Do you really think it could be a paradise parrot?" asked Alexis.

"I'll need to do some research, but this is very intriguing. How old are you girls again?" Evie asked, laughing.

"We're both ten," I said. "We make a really great team," I added, as Alexis put her arm over my shoulder.

"Well, if I find anything, you two will be the first to know," said Evie. "I mean, it would be the discovery of a lifetime. Just think how exciting that would be!" She beamed at Auntie Lynette.

"Two kids and a PhD student discover an extinct bird on the Bailey Wildlife Sanctuary," said Aunt Mamie. "Sounds like a major news story to me!"

GOODBYES
Chapter 17

Early the next morning, I ventured out of our warm tent and into the dark and silent bush camp. Quietly, I took a piece of leftover bacon from the cooler. Instead of heading for the swing on the veranda, I went straight to the shed, where Mr. Curry kept the animal crates. I found a wire cage trap and took it back to the farmhouse.

The orange cat came out of the bush when it saw me walking down the path. I set the trap on the lawn near the veranda, opened the door, and put some bacon inside. Then I added a little trail of bacon pieces leading to the trap. I sat down beside it and waited.

When the cat saw the strange new object next to me, he retreated into the bush.

"Come on, kitty." I patted the grass in front of me. "You just can't stay here. We'll find a better home for you, where you'll have plenty of food to eat." *And where you can't harm any wild animals,* I added in my head.

The cat couldn't resist the easy breakfast. He inched closer and closer to the trap, eating up the bits of bacon I had laid out. I held my breath, not making a single move as he put one orange paw inside the cage. The cat stretched his body very long, sniffing around inside, probably smelling wombat or possum or bandicoot. And bacon. They must have been his favorite smells, because he went all the way in and began to eat the big piece of bacon I'd set there.

Quietly, I released the catch, and the wire door dropped down. Bingo.

A moment later, Auntie Lynette and Mom came out of the farmhouse with cups of coffee. They halted when they saw me on the lawn. Inside the cage, the cat hissed at them.

"You caught the cat! Bravo!" Auntie Lynette exclaimed.

"Yep." I stood up and brushed dry grass off my clothes. "I'm starving. Is it time for breakfast?"

"You caught a cat and it's barely seven in the morning?" Mom looked at her watch, chuckling. "You're becoming more and more like your Aunt Mamie every day." She gave me a sideways squeeze, kissing my head until I squirmed out of her arms.

"Where is Aunt Mamie, anyway?" I asked.

"Taking her time getting up," Mom said. "She'll meet you at the clinic in an hour."

My stomach twinged. Today was the day we were taking Bean to the koala sanctuary.

Auntie Lynette lifted the cage, with the cat still in it, and set it in the back of the land rover. "After you deliver Bean, you can pop in at the RSPCA and drop off the cat. They'll take care of it.

I nodded. RSPCA stood for Royal Society for the Prevention of Cruelty to Animals. In Australia, the RSPCA is like the Humane Society in the United States.

Auntie Lynette closed the hatch on the rover and dusted off her hands. "Glad that's done with. Now, back to the bush camp for brekky."

At the bush camp, everyone was already at the picnic table. As we ate our eggs on toast, I told them how I had lured the cat into the trap with bacon, and everyone cheered and clinked glasses of orange juice to celebrate the capture of the predator. Secretly, I couldn't help feeling a bit sorry for the cat, knowing his days of roaming free were over, but I was glad he couldn't endanger any more wildlife.

After breakfast, Alexis and I walked to the clinic.

"Are you sure you don't want to come with us?" I asked. "You can hold Bean in the car if you want."

Alexis patted my back. "Thanks, mate, but I think Bean needs you."

Bean was all packed up and ready to go when I got there. Mrs. Curry gave him one last hug, and Alexis kissed his little ears and petted his fuzzy head.

"Big day for such a small bean," Mrs. Curry said, putting him in my arms.

I carried Bean and his supply bag, and Aunt Mamie and I walked carefully to the driveway, where Mom waited for us by the land rover. As we passed Dodger's cage, I was surprised to see that not only was the magpie gone, but his enclosure had been completely cleaned up and cleared out.

"He finally took the plunge," Aunt Mamie said. "He just needed some extra time."

I knew how Dodger felt. It wasn't easy going from a place that felt like home—a safe, familiar place with plenty of food and friends—to a strange new place where you weren't sure what was going to happen next. A place where good food was scarce, friends were few and far between, and predators—or bullies—might be lurking around the corner. A place like the Australian bush . . . or middle school. But if Dodger could do it, if Bean could do it, then I figured I could do it, too.

I sat in the backseat of the car with Bean snuggled in my arms. "I'm going to miss you so much, my little Bean," I whispered to the baby koala. He tilted his head out of his blanket when he heard my voice. "But you'll love the new place. Koalas are their specialty, and they have a big enclosure set up for you outside in the middle of a gum forest, with all the eucalyptus leaves a koala could want."

GOODBYES

I scratched him between his ears. "I have to go home anyway in six weeks, to get ready for middle school. And you have to get ready to be released someday and become a wild koala."

Bean looked up at me, and I wiped my eyes. "I know, I know. It's not going to be easy for either of us. But you'll make new friends, don't worry." I stroked his head. "Give the other koalas a chance, and when it's time to go out into the wild forest, you'll be ready."

And before I knew it, we were pulling into a parking lot surrounded by silvery eucalyptus trees. This was it. I clutched Bean tighter.

Aunt Mamie opened my door. "Straight on. Let's go and set Bean on his way to freedom."

I swallowed the lump in my throat and stepped out of the car as a man in khaki shorts walked over to meet us. I took a breath, quickly thinking of happy things. A kangaroo's long eyelashes. A koala's tufted ears and button nose. A cat's rumbling purr. While the adults talked, I memorized every detail of Bean—his thick gray fur, sweet eyes that melted my heart, and faint eucalyptus smell.

Aunt Mamie was right that the hardest part of being an animal rescuer was when you had to say goodbye to an animal you loved. But now I knew that loving Bean meant I had to let him go. So I faced it, straight on. With one more

GOODBYES

kiss, a scratch under his chin, and a promise to never forget him, I handed Bean to the man, along with a piece of my heart.

Walking back to the car, Aunt Mamie squeezed my hand. "I'm proud of you, bunny. You did good."

I squeezed her hand too, not looking back. Instead I forced myself to think ahead, like how I still had the rest of the summer to work in the clinic, hang out with Alex, and maybe even find a very rare parrot.

Bean had taught me so much. How to feed a stubborn joey. How to cuddle a koala just right. But the most important lesson I learned from Bean was this one: that even though helping animals wasn't easy—even though sometimes it hurt—it was totally worth it.

DISCUSSION GUIDE

1. Kira's friend from school, Laila, told Kira she should "go with the flow." Do you agree with Laila? Was Laila right to say such a thing to her friend?

2. Why does Kira envy Alexis? And why does Alexis become jealous of Kira? Have you ever felt jealous toward a good friend because she had something you wished for?

3. Auntie Lynette and her students talk about the drought and fires in Australia. Do you know some other places in the world that are having unusual weather and natural disasters like drought, floods, fires, or ice melt?

4. Kira learns that the hardest part of raising and caring for animals is letting them go once they are ready. Do you agree with her? What other aspects of animal care do you think would be difficult?

Koala
Girl

Bonding with baby koalas is an everyday event for the Bee family.

Izzy and her
favorite patient,
Princess Leia

126

Imagine growing up with koalas in your house! Twelve-year-old Isabella Bee, who goes by Izzy, shares her home with koalas that she and her parents are nursing back to health. Izzy feeds and plays with the koalas and often forms a special bond with the joeys.

"There are very few times that we don't have koala joeys living in the house with us, in the koala nursery," says Izzy's mother, Dr. Alison Bee, a veterinarian. "I will find them all happily watching TV, Izzy with one baby on her lap and one on her head in her hair!"

Alison, who goes by Ali, started out treating mostly dogs, cats, and birds at her veterinary clinic in northern Queensland, Australia. She began bringing home koalas who were orphaned and needed more time and care before they could be released. At one point, there were thirteen koalas living at Izzy's house! "Baby koalas are like humans and they love their mums," explains Izzy. "They are really sad and scared after they have lost their mums."

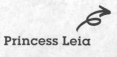
Princess Leia

127

Crikey

Crikey was a young koala who had lost his mother. He was grieving, depressed, and refusing to eat. But within minutes of meeting Izzy, he snuggled up with her and began taking the formula she offered him. "Izzy was Crikey's mum as far as he was concerned," says Ali.

Izzy's parents realized the koalas needed a bigger facility, so in 2014 they started the Magnetic Island Koala Hospital to rescue and rehabilitate koalas that are sick, injured, or orphaned. Koalas are affected by drought, fire, and habitat loss as well as viruses and infections, so vets and volunteers are working hard to save them. Izzy's jobs include inspecting and calming the koala patients, feeding older koalas the eucalyptus, or gum tree, leaves that they eat, and preparing special food and formula for the joeys, whom she feeds by hand with a plastic syringe.

"Growing up with koalas, Izzy instinctively knows how to calm the anxious patients down," says Ali. Some people call Izzy

a "koala whisperer" to describe her special bond with them. Her father, Tim, sums it up: "Izzy loves the koalas, and they love her."

Izzy's favorite part of working with koalas is "watching the babies grow up, and the sick and injured ones get strong again and able to be released. I want to help koalas get back on their feet and have a great life" in the wild.

Dr. Alison Bee and Izzy Bee

MEET AUTHOR
Erin Teagan

Erin Teagan loves sharing the most interesting parts of science with kids. She lives in Virginia with her family, a hound dog named Beaker, and a bunny. To write Kira's story, Erin traveled to Australia to learn about the country. Here, she tells about her trip to Walkabout Wildlife Park.

WHAT DID YOU DO AT WALKABOUT PARK?

I helped prepare food for the animals: chopping fresh vegetables, collecting eucalyptus branches, mixing formula for the echidnas, and scattering fruit for the parrots. I even got to bottle-feed a joey wallaby that a ranger was raising! I also helped clean the enclosures of several animals, raking leaves and debris, refreshing food and water, and checking the animals to make sure they were healthy.

I stayed overnight in the park, in a little bungalow that overlooked a circle of tents. We went spotlighting with a ranger when it was dark, using our flashlights to find animals. We saw

a roosting peacock in a tree, owls, bats, and possums. Afterward, we had a campfire and roasted marshmallows.

WHAT KINDS OF ANIMALS DID YOU SEE THERE?

I met a sleepy koala and a hissing bilby, an echidna, a snake, and a huge wombat. I spent time with possums and noisy parrots, one of which screamed "Mother!" every time we passed his pen. While I ate a snack on the veranda, wallabies chased each other around, kangaroos ate from the hay feeders, and emus poked their heads into wheelbarrows full of veggie scraps.

A wombat

HOW DID YOUR TRIP HELP YOU WRITE KIRA'S STORY?

To make sure that the details were accurate, I took pictures of everything: the animals, the enclosures, even the menus for each of the sanctuary's resident animals. I took pictures of where the rangers prepped food, the shed where they kept the eucalyptus branches, and the shelves of supplies. I took videos of the animals so I'd remember how an echidna walked, or how the kangaroos lounged around the park, or how a joey popped out of his mother's pouch.

WHAT DO YOU HOPE READERS TAKE AWAY FROM KIRA'S STORY?

While I was there, the big topic of conversation was the bushfires and how animals are affected. This was hard to hear. But I also learned how animals are tough and resilient. I heard stories about how animals were able to seek shelter from the flames and sometimes even help other animals find safety, such as wombats letting other animals use their underground tunnels (something that doesn't happen ordinarily). I also heard endless stories of koalas and kangaroos and wallabies being taken in by humans during a bushfire. I heard stories of kids raising money for animals in need and knitting pouches for joeys who had lost their mothers. Most of all, I learned that even one kid can make a big difference in an animal's life.

WHAT ELSE DID YOU DO THAT HELPED YOU WRITE KIRA'S STORY?

Instead of staying in hotels, I stayed in homes and got to know my hosts. One host took me on a hike through the bush. His house was in the middle of a gum forest, full of wildlife. He fed the kookaburras on his veranda at night and gave me a bowl of seeds so the parrots would visit me on my balcony. He also told me how he kept his house safe from bushfire. I lingered in the cafés and listened to the conversations around me. By the time my visit was over, I knew a lot more Australian slang and stories, and I had made many new friends.

Erin Teagan feeds a kangaroo joey

A SNEAK PEAK AT
Kira's Animal Rescue

When I finished feeding the baby possums, I found Alexis outside by the supply shed with Blossom, who was bouncing around in the grass.

"She's out of her pouch!" I exclaimed.

Alexis beamed like a proud mama. Blossom was shaky on her big kangaroo feet, jumping haphazardly, once leaping so high that Alexis grabbed her out of the air before she could fall. "Whoa now," she said with a laugh. "Let's go easy, big girl."

I sat next to Alexis and took out my binoculars, scanning the field filled with kangaroos and wallabies grazing. At the far end of the paddock, I could see the path out to the bush and the dense trees beyond. The sanctuary was full of wildlife, a paradise for animals. If the paradise parrot still lived, surely it would live here . . .

"Do you think we'll ever find the paradise parrot?" Alexis asked me, as if she could tell what I was thinking.

"Yes," I said, without hesitation. "Evie says it just requires patience." I smirked at her. "Guess that will be easier for some of us."

She threw a handful of grass at me. "Well, maybe you and Evie just let me know when you find it. I'll do all the fun stuff like feeding the animals, while you sit birdwatching in the bush for hours and hours and hours and—"

"Alex." I was looking through my binoculars again, focusing on a bit of haziness in the sky out in the distance.

"Alex."

"What is it?" she asked, holding out a few blades of grass for Blossom to nibble.

I lowered my binoculars. "It almost looks like smoke. Way out there."

"What?" She stood up, lifting Blossom back into her pouch and reaching out to take a turn with the binoculars.

I hoped that I was wrong, because if there was one thing Auntie Lynette had told us, it was that the sanctuary was ripe for a fire. She said the fuel load—the dry brush, grass, and leaves all over the paddock and forest floor—was high.

Alex sucked in a breath. She saw the smoke, too. A moment later, we heard sirens, and a fire truck peeled into the farmhouse driveway.

MORE FUN WITH GIRL OF THE YEAR

Visit **americangirl.com/play**
to discover more about Kira's world.

Meet Joss Kendrick, a surfer and cheerleader.
Available in stores and online. Each sold separately.

Parents, request a FREE catalogue at
americangirl.com/catalogue.

Sign up at **americangirl.com/email**
to receive the latest news and exclusive offers.